Solving for M

Illustrations by

Jennifer Naalchigar

Jennifer Swender

Solving for M

Crown Books for Young Readers
NEW YORK

Text copyright © 2019 by Jennifer Swender
Jacket art copyright © 2019 by Jim Tierney
Interior illustrations copyright © 2019 by Jennifer Naalchigar

All rights reserved. Published in the United States by Crown Books
for Young Readers, an imprint of Random House Children's Books,
a division of Penguin Random House LLC, New York.

Crown and the colophon are registered trademarks
of Penguin Random House LLC.

Visit us on the Web! rhcbooks.com

Educators and librarians, for a variety of teaching tools,
visit us at RHTeachersLibrarians.com

Library of Congress Cataloging-in-Publication Data is available upon request.
ISBN 978-1-101-93290-2 (trade) — ISBN 978-1-101-93291-9 (lib. bdg.) —
ISBN 978-1-101-93292-6 (ebook)

Interior design by Leslie Mechanic

Printed in the United States of America
10 9 8 7 6 5 4 3 2 1
First Edition

Random House Children's Books supports the First Amendment
and celebrates the right to read.

For Becca

Solving for M

Unit 1

Estimation

Fifth grade at the middle school should make perfect sense.

Elementary school is first grade, second grade, third, and fourth. (Okay, I know I'm leaving out kindergarten, but stick with me for a second.) Then middle school is fifth, sixth, seventh, and eighth. High school—ninth, tenth, eleventh, and twelfth.

Twelve grades divided by three schools gives you four grades per school, with middle school smack dab in the . . . well, middle. Everything nice and logical.

But now, on the first day, I'm not so sure.

First of all, we have to keep a journal . . . in *math*?

Dan P. raises his hand. "Aren't journals supposed to be for language arts?" he asks with a smirk. "Or Gothy kids who want to be poets?"

I know Dan well. He was in my class last year.

Mr. Vann, the math teacher, doesn't say anything as he writes on the board: **Bring in spiral notebook for your math journal. This step is mandatory.** Then he turns back around to the class with a dramatic flourish.

Mr. Vann reminds me of some kind of wacky magician. A cape and top hat would not seem entirely out of the question. He wears these thick glasses that make his eyes look very big and very far away at the same time. And he's left-handed, which means he can write on the board with his left hand as he erases the board with his right. The letters look like they're running to fill up the newly emptied space.

I'm not exactly sure why we need a math journal, but it's not the kind of question I'm going to raise my hand and ask on the first day of middle school. I'll leave that to Dan.

"Why do we need a math journal?" Dan calls out.

"Keeping a math journal will help us transparently tackle innovative problems," Mr. Vann begins. "Keeping a math journal will let us embark on reflective discussions of relevant math issues." He underlines *math journal* on the board every time he says it. "Keeping a math journal will allow us to explore, justify, argue, wonder. . . ."

Well, okay then. I guess that's why you need a math journal. Mr. Vann seems very excited by the whole idea. I bet when Mr. Vann was in fifth grade he kept a math journal without even being asked to. Maybe he invented the math journal.

It's not that I have anything against math. I'm just not much of a math person. It doesn't seem like something to get that excited about. Numbers are numbers, right?

My mom says she likes numbers because you always know what you're going to get with them. She's an accountant, so I guess she should know.

And it's not that I have anything against journals, either. I have like twenty blank books at home. Some are full; some are empty. Some have pages torn out; some have pages stuffed in. But those are for art, not for math.

"Keeping a math journal will allow us to dare to color outside the lines," Mr. Vann adds. Then he spins back around to write something else on the board: Bring in colored pencils and/or markers for your math journal. This step is optional.

I guess he wasn't kidding about the coloring part. And I can get excited about anything that involves colored pencils and/or markers—drawing, doodling, sketching. I can do horses really well, and I'm pretty good at people, too. I have a book that shows how to draw things in a certain number of steps. You just follow the directions and everything turns out the way it's supposed to.

"What do we need colored pencils for?" Dan asks.

"Patience, please, my dear Watson," Mr. Vann says. Then he opens the top drawer of his desk and takes out a box of matches. I'm half expecting him to light a pipe. But instead, he reaches into the drawer again and takes out what looks like a white tea candle.

Is he allowed to have candles and matches in school? I'm pretty sure that's got to be against the middle school rules.

Mr. Vann dramatically strikes the match on the box and lights the candle. "Remember, dear thinkers," he says. "Math may be exact."

Then he blows out the candle, pops it into his mouth, and eats it.

"But life is mostly estimation."

Before anyone can say anything, the bell rings (although the middle school bell sounds more like a horn), and Mr. Vann dismisses us to the auditorium. There's a welcome assembly for the fifth grade.

Am I the only one thinking that first thing this morning might have been a better time for a welcome assembly? Anyway, we all file in and find our seats.

Principal Mir walks to the microphone. You can hear her shoes going click, click, click across the shiny floor.

Principal Mir is a small woman, but she has the look of someone you do *not* want to mess with. She's wearing a matching plaid skirt and jacket and very sensible shoes.

"Welcome to Highbridge Middle School," she begins. "Pride of the Upper Hudson Valley. We hope you had no trouble finding your pods this morning."

I should explain that a pod is a team of teachers, all in the same hallway. My mom says they put the fifth graders into pods to make the middle school feel smaller and less overwhelming.

I suddenly get this funny picture in my mind of all of us fifth graders as space aliens who have just arrived on this strange new planet called Highbridge Middle. Luckily, we have our home pods to make us feel safe and cozy.

Across the auditorium, I see Ella, my best friend from fourth grade. I wave to her, but she's whispering to the girl sitting next to her and doesn't see me.

I'm in Pod Two. Ella is in Pod One. I guess we can still probably eat lunch together, but besides that, we're on totally opposite ends of the building for the whole day. So even though the pods are supposed to make you feel safe and cozy, they mostly make you feel like your friends are far away.

Principal Mir goes on and on about middle school rules, and how the rules are there to keep us healthy and safe. I wonder if she has any idea about the fire hazard that just took place in Grade Five Pod Two Math Block C.

Then she explains about A-days and B-days, and twice-a-month early-dismissal days, and once-a-quarter late-start days. "Fifth graders have physical education every other day," she tells us. "Remember proper footwear, please. That is, unless you are a member of the chorus or the jazz band, of course. Then you will always have physical education on Tuesdays and Thursdays, unless there's an impending concert or unusually inclement weather."

Should somebody be writing this down?

"Upon dismissal from assembly," Principal Mir continues, "please return to your Home Pod Block C, which is the class you would normally have directly following lunch, for immediate dismissal to the buses."

I'm starting to think that fifth grade at the middle school might not make very much sense at all.

"I still don't know about having fifth graders at the middle school," Mom says as she takes my backpack from me. I can't believe she walked out to the corner to wait for my bus. She's the only parent here.

"Everybody else's parents let them walk home alone," I whisper.

"Good thing I'm not everybody else's parent," she says, ruffling my hair. "*That* would be exhausting." It's one of my mom's favorite comebacks. "So?" she asks in her trying-not-to-be-nosy way. "How was it?"

"It was fine," I say. "A little weird. I mean, it wasn't a normal day. They changed the schedule all around. We had a welcome assembly last thing in the afternoon. And we have to keep a journal in math. And Ella's in Pod One."

"I'm sure you'll make some new friends," Mom says with extra corny sauce added for good measure. I give that comment an exaggerated eye roll.

"And of course, Dan P. is in *all* of my classes," I tell her. Mom gives her own eye roll back.

"Nothing a little time won't help," she says, sounding like a very reasonable television psychologist. "I'm sure it will sort itself out."

I guess she's right. Maybe it's something you have to get used to—all these different people in different combinations at different times. In elementary school, it was always the same kids, same teacher, all day, every day. And at home, it's just Mom and me—same combination, all the time.

"Just the girls," Mom likes to say. Or "Just the two of us." Then she starts singing that sappy song: *Just the two of us. We can make it if we try!* We can't even have a dog or cat because my mom is allergic. I had a goldfish once, but it didn't last very long.

My dad has always not been around, so it's never seemed like that big a deal. My parents got divorced before I was even one. "That decision was set in motion long before you were on the scene" is my mom's go-to line on that topic.

My dad lives in Florida with his new wife, Katie, and their dogs. I go there for two weeks in the summer, and he comes to New York for work meetings and stuff a couple of times a year.

Sometimes I think Mom and I were like his rough-draft family—the same way we have to write rough drafts in language arts. Then he went through the revision process and moved someplace warmer.

Math Journal Entry #1

Karina is 11. Her mother is 38. Karina says that her mother is approximately 40 years older than she is. Is her statement reasonable?

Explain your thinking using words, numbers, and/or pictures.

"Who would like to share their answer to the first math journal challenge?" Mr. Vann asks on approximately the sixth day of school. A couple of kids raise their hands.

I'm starting to learn the names of the kids in this class and every other class. And it's a lot of kids. Our school district has four elementary schools, each with three fourth-grade classes. Then we all get mixed up for fifth grade. Maybe Mr. Vann should make a math journal "challenge" out of that.

A girl named Chelsea raises her hand so high it looks like she's going to pop her shoulder right out of the socket. Chelsea's in my art class and my gym class. She raises her hand a lot, even in gym, and she keeps all of her notebooks organized in the biggest three-ring binder I have ever seen.

Chelsea reads from her math journal very slowly. "Karina's mother is twenty-seven years older than she is." Then she looks up. "It's pretty easy subtraction. You don't even have to borrow."

"Regroup!" Mr. Vann shouts, snapping his fingers on both hands. "Neither a borrower nor a lender be, please. Elementary school, Chelsea?" he asks with raised eyebrows.

I can see that Chelsea is confused. I can also see that she's not used to *not* getting the right answer.

"Pardon?" she says.

"No, don't tell me." Mr. Vann paces in front of the board, with a dry-erase marker stuck in the corner of his mouth. "Mrs. Henneberry at Montgomery Hills," he announces, holding the marker high above his head.

"She was my teacher last year!" Chelsea says, all bright again.

"Yes, she was," says Mr. Vann. "And you have given us the correct answer, dear Chelsea."

Chelsea takes a deep breath to settle down her popped-out shoulder. Now she's *really* smiling.

"The correct answer," Mr. Vann continues, "to the wrong question. Who would care to elaborate?"

Dan P. raises his hand.

"The correct answer is that Karina is totally unreasonable," Dan says with a smirk. "I think she might be a little crazy." He circles his pointer finger in the air by his ear.

Everybody giggles. I can tell that Dan is waiting to see what Mr. Vann will do.

"I asked for elaboration, not psychological evaluation, Mr. Pimental. When you receive your doctorate in psychology, we will revisit the question of our dear Karina's mental health." Mr. Vann gets the bigger laugh.

"Why do we even need to know?" someone mutters from the back of the room.

Mr. Vann's shoulders slump. "Dear thinkers," he says like he's suddenly very disappointed in all of us. "It is *always* better to know. Now, who would care to share?"

A kid named Miles raises his hand and explains how eleven rounds down to ten, and thirty-eight rounds up to forty, and how you subtract one from the other, and that Karina's statement is, in fact, *not* reasonable.

Mr. Vann listens and nods as he walks through the rows of desks. I'm pretty sure he's walking around the room with his eyes closed. I don't understand how he's not bumping into things. Then he stops behind Miles's shoulder just as Miles finishes talking.

"And yet, Miles," Mr. Vann responds, "in your math journal, I see only the number forty, a sign indicating subtraction, the number ten, a sign indicating equality, the number thirty, and the word *No*.

"People!" Mr. Vann practically shouts as he runs to the front of the room. "I am giving you an opportunity—the invaluable opportunity to explain your thinking." He knocks on the board under the words Explain your thinking.

"You will find that it is an opportunity not that often granted. Seize it." He clenches his hands into fists and gets very quiet. "As did our dear Mika."

I look up, surprised by the sound of my name. I'm also surprised that Mr. Vann pronounced it correctly. (The first syllable sounds like "me," but sometimes people say it like "my.")

It's not like I solved the problem in some super-interesting way. Maybe Mr. Vann liked that I mentioned his candle trick. Or maybe he liked that I explained my thinking using words, numbers, *and* pictures. I used my *How to Draw People* book to get the mother and the daughter just right.

Truth is, I haven't had a chance to do much drawing in any of my other classes lately, not even art. Mrs. Poole, the middle school art teacher, has explained several times that the fifth-grade curriculum does not include drawing. Whenever she says the word *drawing,* she makes those fake quotation marks in the air with her fingers. Instead, the fifth-grade curriculum focuses on found materials. We're currently making collages out of things we find outside.

But wait a second. How did Mr. Vann see my math journal entry, anyway? All I can think is that he saw it when he was walking around the room with his eyes closed.

"So, why do we estimate?" Mr. Vann asks next.

Chelsea pops her shoulder up again and starts talking before she's even called on. "Key words for estimation are *about, approximately,* and *to the nearest.*" She smiles.

"I cannot argue with you," Mr. Vann begins. "And yet I wish you would refrain from answering the question you *think* I am asking in favor of the question that I *am* asking." He doesn't say it meanly, more like a polite request. I can't help laughing a little, but Chelsea doesn't seem to get it.

Then Mr. Vann starts erasing the math journal question with his right hand as he writes with his left hand: We estimate when . . .

"You are going to work in groups to complete this statement," he announces. I end up with Miles, Chelsea, and a girl named Dee Dee. I stay quiet as they talk about what our group should say.

Math Journal Entry #2

Last year, Maxwell Elementary had 68 fourth graders, Garcia Elementary had 77 fourth graders, Montgomery Hills had 71 fourth graders, and Bishop Street School had 77 fourth graders. Assuming that no students moved in or moved away, approximately how many students are in this year's fifth-grade class?

Explain your thinking using words, numbers, and/or pictures.

80 + 70 + 80 + 70 = approximately 300 very mixed-up fifth graders!

Mr. Vann asks for our thoughts on the latest math journal quandary.

"What about kids who flunked?" Dan shouts out. "You told us nobody moved away, but you didn't say anything about flunkers."

Mr. Vann nods. "I am proud to announce that all of last year's fourth graders are currently enrolled at Highbridge Middle School. Whether the same will be said of this year's fifth graders, we will have to wait and see." That shuts Dan up for the rest of class.

Mr. Vann says we don't ever have to hand our math journals in. They're a private place to record our thoughts and processes. But he does walk around a lot and look over our shoulders while we discuss the answers.

I don't know how Mr. Vann knew I was thinking about this particular math journal "quandary," but I liked drawing the answer. I had extra time to work on it in the cafeteria before class.

Even though it doesn't make a lot of sense, I think the hardest part of middle school is lunch. There are dozens of starving aliens trying to locate nourishment and find an acceptable place to ingest it.

I thought Ella and I were so lucky to have the same lunch period, but the way things work out, Pod One is usually halfway finished before Pod Two even makes it to the start of the line.

By the time I got through the line today, Ella was already cleaning up her tray. Plus, she was sitting with a bunch of girls from Pod One who I don't even know, and there were no empty seats at the table.

"You can have my seat, Mika," Ella said, standing up. All the other girls stood up, too.

"Tomorrow we should wear blue pants and green shirts," one of them said.

"And purple hair ties!" another one suggested.

"We have a new club," the first girl explained. "The Onesies!"

"Because we're in Pod One," Ella said with a little shrug.

They left to go bus their trays and head outside. I pretended like it was taking all of my concentration just to open my milk carton. Then I took out my math journal and worked on my aliens a little longer.

Unit 2

Time

We've moved on to time in math, even though time is covered at the end of chapter four.

"When a topic becomes relevant," Mr. Vann explains, "that is obviously the best time to explore it." Everyone has been coming to math late, so Mr. Vann has decided that time is a relevant topic.

It's not our fault. Math comes right after lunch, and when you've finished eating, you can go outside. They don't call it recess because this is middle school, after all. But most kids wolf down their food and then head outside to play Frisbee or soccer or just hang out.

And you can't blame people for not wanting to come back inside for class. It's still "warm as toast," as my mom likes to say. The sky is that shade of blue that seems clearer in the fall, and the light slants at interesting angles.

Today, the clouds look like cotton balls that somebody pulled apart and tossed up into the air, like something Monet would paint. Take a look at his *Village Street* painting. That's the kind of sky I mean. All wispy and soft and exactly right.

Monet is probably my favorite artist, and I know for a fact that he spent a fair amount of his time "drawing." Over the summer, Mom and I went to a museum in Utica. They had a traveling exhibit of all the French Impressionists.

My favorite painting there wasn't by Monet, though. It was by an artist I'd never heard of before—Morisot. *Peasant Girl Among Tulips.*

I spent a long time just staring at that girl's face. She was sitting in a bunch of flowers with her hands clasped together, looking like she was waiting for something, or maybe somebody. The colors of the flowers matched the colors in her dress, and her face was the same shade of peach as the tulips.

"What do you think she's thinking about?" Mom asked me.

I didn't say anything. I didn't really have an answer.

"Maybe about what middle school is going to be like?" she asked next.

I knew Mom was just trying to "check in," as she says, but I had to give her an extra-exaggerated eye roll for that one.

"I'm pretty sure she doesn't go to middle school," I said.

19

Math Journal Entry #3

Think about something you experienced recently. Estimate when the activity began and when it ended. Then figure the elapsed time spent on the activity to the nearest quarter hour.

Explain your thinking using words, numbers, and/or pictures.

I finished looking at Peasant Girl Among Tulips at 2:18 p.m.

I started looking at Peasant Girl Among Tulips at 2:00 p.m.

To estimate, I looked at Peasant Girl Among Tulips for $\frac{1}{4}$ of an hour.

2:00

2:18

(But I still don't know what she was thinking about.)

Dan P. says that we can easily solve our coming-to-math-late problem by having class outside. That way, kids can just stay outside after lunch and they won't be late for math.

Mr. Vann surprises everybody by saying, "Makes perfect sense."

We all follow Mr. Vann through the side doors and sit in a big circle on the grass. It's funny to see the classroom from the outside. It looks so empty.

Mr. Vann holds up a stack of paper plates. "One to a customer," he says in a silly voice, like he's hawking games at a county fair. Then he asks Dee Dee to pass them out.

Dee Dee was in my discussion group for the estimation unit. She's also in my science class, and she is *really* into science. She always wears these T-shirts with funny science stuff on them. Today, her shirt says: *Don't trust atoms. They make up everything.*

Dee Dee tosses me my plate like a Frisbee. Then she gives me a thumbs-up.

Mr. Vann takes a thick black marker out of his pocket. He draws a point in the middle of his paper plate. Then he draws two arrows pointing directly up. One is shorter than the other.

"What is the time?" he asks.

Dan looks at his watch and yells out, "One-eighteen."

I'm not about to raise my hand and point out that coming outside in order to save time has actually made us start class a full eleven minutes late. It's fun sitting crisscross-applesauce on the grass. It's warm as toast, and I like feeling the sun on my face.

"Willing suspension of disbelief," Mr. Vann replies. "Please give me the time represented by my theatrical stage prop, not the *real* time."

A boy named Malcolm raises his hand. "Twelve o'clock," he says.

"Twelve a.m. or p.m.?" Mr. Vann says with one eyebrow raised. It's the look of someone asking a trick question.

"Beats me," Malcolm says with a shrug.

"Correct!" Mr. Vann shouts. Then he starts howling like a wolf or a coyote. "The moon, the moon," he calls, holding up another paper plate to play the part.

Mr. Vann can be really goofy, but the funny thing is, because he's the one goofing off, none of the kids do.

"Twelve o'clock a.m.," Malcolm says.

"Correct again!" Mr. Vann yells.

Then he takes out a pair of teacher scissors and starts cutting his plate into different sections to show us how fifteen minutes is the same as one-quarter of a plate, and thirty minutes is the same as one-half of a plate—if you remember that the plate is a clock, that is.

Chelsea tentatively raises her hand. "Um," she starts. "Is this *actually* part of the fifth-grade curriculum? I mean, we made plate-clocks in second grade."

"Oh, we're not making plate-clocks," Mr. Vann says with a chuckle. "Although that is an *excellent* idea." He takes a scrap of paper out of his pocket, jots a note on it, and puts it back. "We are visually representing fractional parts of a whole using the two-dimensional form of a circle."

He pauses because he realizes we're all pretty confused. "We're gonna cut the plates up!" he says enthusiastically.

Of course, nobody thought to bring scissors when we came outside, so the cutting part is a definite challenge. Kids start folding and ripping their plates, or just coloring in the different sections. I take out my colored pencils.

First, I divide my plate in half and then in half again. I color each quarter a different shade of blue. Then I divide each quarter into three equal parts (each representing five minutes, of course).

I leave the two sections on the outside plain blue. But in the center sections, I use my eraser to make clouds. It's like taking the color away to leave the white. It gets all smudged and blurry, but I like the way it comes out, kind of like a Monet sky.

"That is so cool," Dee Dee says, pointing down at my plate.

"Thanks," I say.

This is more like art than what we did in art today, which was walking through the field to collect rocks and acorns. That was more like science. But in science, we wrote poems about the circulatory system, which was more like language arts. If I'd had music today, we probably would have played a good game of soccer.

★ ★ ★

When I get home from school, I take my oil pastels and one of my blank books, and I go outside to draw for a while. I'm trying to get the color of the leaves. They're not all red and orange and yellow yet, but they've changed a little bit, like someone started turning down the dimmer on their light.

I barely get started when Mom calls me inside. I know I'm not doing my homework "first things first." (Mom always says it's important to do your must-do's before your may-do's.) But usually if I'm drawing, she doesn't care that much.

"Mika!" I hear again. I gather up my stuff and head inside.

"I have a doctor's appointment," she tells me.

"What?" I say. "Now?"

I am totally confused. I should explain that my mom makes a to-do list every day. She has a pad of paper with a magnet on the back of it that sticks to the fridge. It says To-Do Today in swirly letters at the top. Below that, she writes the date, and then she makes a list of everything that's "on tap" for the day.

To be exact, she makes *two* lists—one for her and one for me. But my list only ever has the same three things on it: 1) Make bed. 2) Go to school. 3) Do homework.

If my mom had an appointment, it would have been on the fridge, and I would have known about it.

"This was not on the list today," I say, shaking my finger and making a face like I'm the parent and she is in really big trouble.

"They squeezed me in last minute," she explains.

It seems like there should be an easy comeback to that, but I can't think of one at the moment. I open the fridge and look around. Maybe I'll grab a snack for the road.

"Mika, fridge," Mom says. Mom gets on my case for holding the refrigerator door open. "One of the largest avoidable utility expenses," she likes to remind me.

I close the door. "Why do you have to go to the doctor, anyway?" I ask.

"Oh, I just noticed a spot on my leg that looks a little strange," she says.

"You always look a little strange," I say, making a silly face.

Usually Mom would make her own silly face back, and follow it up with: "I know you're strange, but what am I?" But she doesn't say anything.

"Why can't I stay home?" I ask.

One problem with it being "just the girls" is that wherever Mom goes, I have to go, too. "Everybody else's parents let them stay home alone," I try.

Mom delivers her expected "Good thing I'm not everybody else's parent." But when she says it, something weird happens. Her voice cracks. I'm startled out of my whining.

"Please, Mika," Mom says quietly. "Let's just go, okay?"

I suddenly get this weird feeling at the back of my neck, like someone is squeezing it even though no one is. I drop my drawing stuff on the table, grab my backpack, and head out to the car.

Math Journal Entry #4
A Math Lib

Mika started _waiting_ at _3:36 p.m._ .
(name)   (verb with -ing)   (exact time)

S/he finished _waiting_ at _5:17 p.m._ .
(verb with -ing)   (exact time)

S/he spent _101 minutes_ _waiting_ .
(elapsed time)   (verb with -ing)

My Monet clock

3:36

5:17

"Yankees all-star pitcher Daniel Pimental started pitching the American League Championship's seventh and deciding game at one-oh-seven p.m.," Dan reads out loud from his math journal. "He finished pitching his perfect game at three-fifty-two p.m. He spent two hours and forty-five minutes clinching the American League Championship." Dan ends his Math Lib with a fist pump. Mr. Vann gives him polite applause.

Dee Dee reads next. "Dee Dee started looking through her Orion SpaceProbe Altazimuth Reflector Telescope promptly after school at three-oh-two p.m. She finished looking through her Orion SpaceProbe Altazimuth Reflector Telescope directly before bedtime at twelve-forty-eight a.m. She spent nine hours and forty-six minutes looking through her Orion SpaceProbe Altazimuth Reflector Telescope."

"Very inspiring," Mr. Vann says. "By the way, what kind of telescope do you have?" He winks.

Dee Dee just winks back at him.

"Mika?" Mr. Vann says next. "Care to share? Because remember, to share is to care."

"No, thanks," I mumble.

Maybe if I had done this math journal exploration *before* my mom's doctor appointment instead of *after,* I would have written something different. I wonder if Mr. Vann ever thinks about time that way—how things can turn out differently depending on when you do them.

If I had done my homework first things first (like I was supposed to), I might have written something funny like Dan or clever like Dee Dee. I might have written: *Mika started tap-dancing at three-forty-five p.m. She finished high-kicking at five-forty-six p.m. She spent two hours and one minute perfecting her "Shuffle Off to Buffalo" routine.*

That probably would have gotten a good laugh or maybe even a few bonus points. Mr. Vann is always giving random bonus points for interesting answers, and random demerits for hasty answers. "Fools rush in where angels fear to tread," he likes to remind us.

Instead, I wrote about waiting at the doctor's office because it felt like I was waiting there forever—one hundred and one minutes, to be exact. At least I had plenty of time to work on my drawing.

Mom said she just wanted the doctor to take a quick look, but they must have taken more than that because when we got home, she had a big bandage taped to the back of her knee.

Unit 3

Measurement

"We've spent enough time on time," Mr. Vann announces. "Since it's all relative anyway, we've spent relatively enough time on it. So we're moving ahead to the beginning of chapter four, which, as we are coming from the end of chapter four, is a bit like going back to the future, so in a sense, it seems that we are still contemplating time after all."

Like many things in fifth grade at the middle school, Mr. Vann often makes very little sense. In any case, learning about time wasn't really helping with our coming-to-math-late problem. If anything, it just gave kids funnier excuses.

"I started opening my locker at one-oh-two," Dee Dee says as she hurries in the door. "I couldn't get my locker open until one-oh-nine. I spent seven minutes of elapsed time trying to open my locker. And that's why I'm late."

"I entered the boys' bathroom at one-oh-one," Dan begins.

"I suspect," Mr. Vann interrupts just in time, "that what we are having is not a time problem after all, but a *space* problem." He looks at Dee Dee knowingly. "That is why we're moving back to the beginning of chapter four: measurement."

Everybody flips backward to the correct page in the textbook. Chelsea, who is never late to class, looks particularly confused.

"If our classroom were closer to the cafeteria"— Mr. Vann rubs his chin—"then we might have less difficulty arriving punctually after lunch. Perhaps we should hold math in the janitor's closet directly across from the cafeteria."

I can see Chelsea fussing with the top button of her sweater. She's probably worried about how we're all going to fit into the closet, where she's going to sit, and what we're going to use for a board.

Mr. Vann opens the top drawer of his desk and takes out a bunch of wooden rulers. He spreads them like a fan. "Serious thinkers need serious tools," he says very seriously.

I'm not sure how a wooden ruler is all that serious, but it is better than the cardboard ruler that you punch out of the back of the textbook. Those get all bent and fuzzy.

Mr. Vann starts passing out the rulers. "One to a customer!" everybody shouts.

"Now, let's imagine," Mr. Vann says as he walks around the room, "our dear Dan is catching for the Boston Red Sox." Dan laughs because he's the biggest Yankees fan ever. Plus, he's a pitcher.

Mr. Vann keeps talking and passing out rulers. "And let's say Dan wants to measure the distance from third plate to home base."

"It's third *base* to home *plate*," Dan says with a sigh.

"That's what I said," Mr. Vann says, even though we all know that is not what he said. "What unit of measure would be most appropriate for Dan to use?"

A few kids raise their hands.

"No," Mr. Vann interrupts before he even calls on anyone. "Better scenario. Let's say Dan is dancing with the Joffrey Ballet."

"No way," Dan mutters. But then Chelsea glares at him. I guess Chelsea is into ballet. Good for her.

"Dan needs to measure the distance across the stage to make sure he has ample space to complete his world-famous *grand jeté*. What unit of measure would be most appropriate?" Mr. Vann sits down at his desk and starts opening drawers like he's searching for something.

After a moment, he looks up at us. "Well, go on already," he says as if we are all misbehaving by staying in our seats. "Time to start measuring." He spreads his arms, pointing to the classroom like it's a prize on a game show.

"And please remember to attend to precision, dear

thinkers. If nothing else, measurement is a way for us to get a handle on things. Measurement lets us know exactly where we stand."

When I get home from school, Mom calls me into the living room. (She stopped picking me up at the bus stop.) Then she sits me down on the couch for a big explanation.

The reason my mom came home with a bandage last week is that the doctor had actually taken off the funny-looking spot right then and there. Then they sent a sample to a lab, where someone looked at it under a microscope. And that should have been the end of it.

"It looks as if they found something," Mom begins.

I'm confused. Isn't finding something supposed to be good? Like that time I thought I'd lost my house key, but it was just buried at the bottom of my backpack wrapped up in an old tissue. But it's pretty clear from Mom's voice that this is not the kind of something you want to find.

"It's nothing to worry about," she says with a face that doesn't match her words. "I did a little research, and ninety-six percent of these cases end up perfectly fine."

We haven't gotten to percentages in math yet, but it doesn't take a genius to do the subtraction. What about the other 4 percent? I want to ask. But Mom keeps on talking. It's like she has to get everything off her list, and then she'll be taking questions.

"Next week I'll go back so the doctor can remove a little more," Mom explains. "Just to make sure they got it all."

For someone who usually makes a point of "attending to precision," my mom is being pretty vague. How much is a little more? Exactly how big a deal is this?

"I don't have to stay overnight or anything," she says. "They do it first thing in the morning, and I'll be home by noon." She tells me all of this with a smile on her face, but it's one of those fake, tight parent smiles. Then she hugs me for way too long.

I could use whole minutes to measure the length of that hug. And any hug on a regular school day that lasts for more than a full minute for no apparent reason is just plain weird.

"Jeannie will pick me up around seven," Mom says.

Jeannie is my mom's best friend, even if they are total opposites. My mom is an accountant; Jeannie is an actress. Jeannie says Mom is too predictable; Mom says Jeannie is too unpredictable. The only thing they both agree on is that if they hadn't been stuck together as roommates in college, they never would have become friends. They probably never would have even met.

Mom continues with the plan. "We'll be gone before you have to leave for the bus. So see? You *do* get to stay home by yourself." She says this like it's a huge honor and I'm supposed to be super-duper excited about it. But I know that she knows that staying home by yourself first thing in the morning is not what I was talking about.

Plus, if Jeannie picks my mom up at seven and I leave for the bus at 7:15, that's only fifteen minutes of elapsed home-alone time.

"Think of it like a bad spot on a peach," Mom says. "They just cut it out, and then the peach is as good as new."

Except the peach has a big hole in it, I think. But I don't say it out loud.

Math Journal Entry #5

Think of something, anything, that can be measured.

Describe what unit of measurement you would use to measure it and why.

Explain your thinking using words, numbers, and/or pictures.

I used centimeters and millimeters because that is what the doctors use. They use centimeters and millimeters because these things are pretty small. That's supposed to be good.

They use centimeters and millimeters because they use the metric system. I think because the whole world uses the metric system.

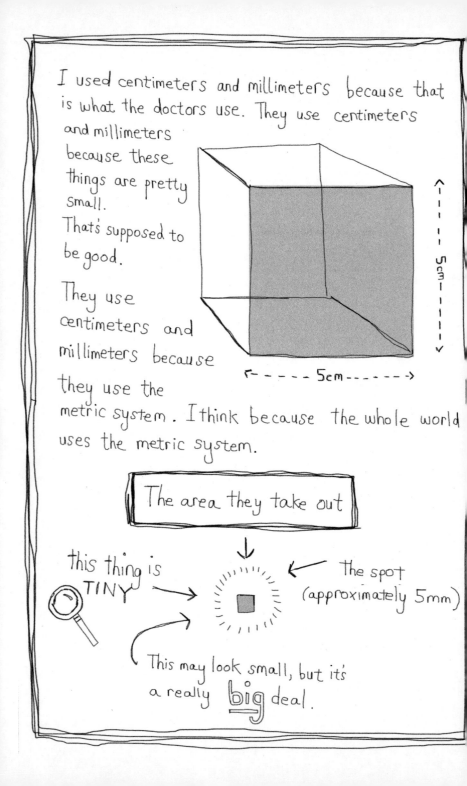

↑ 5cm ↓

← - - - - - 5cm - - - - - →

The area they take out
↓

this thing is TINY →

← the spot (approximately 5mm)

This may look small, but it's a really **big** deal.

I try to find Ella at lunch to see if I can borrow her phone. You're not supposed to have phones in school, even though just about everybody does, except me, of course.

"Whom do you really need to call?" Mom says whenever I ask for one. She always gives an extra-long eye roll when she says the *really* part.

But the person I *really* need to call is her. I want to make sure she's home. The main office has a strict "emergency only" phone policy, and Mom assured me this morning that this procedure was in no way an emergency. Still, I just want to know that she's home and that everything went fine and that everything is back to normal.

I don't see Ella in the cafeteria, so I quickly eat my lunch and head outside. I spot her by the soccer field with the Onesies.

Today, they are wearing blue jeans and purple shirts. As I get closer, I can hear them cracking up like someone just told the funniest joke ever in the history of the universe. I decide to forget about borrowing Ella's phone.

I don't want to go back to the cafeteria, so I head to math early. The door is open.

"Hey, Mika," I hear from the back of the room.

It's Dee Dee. She's sitting at her desk, reading some big encyclopedia-looking book. She sets the book down and gives me a little wave. Her T-shirt today says: *Think like a proton. Stay positive.*

"Oh, hi," I say. "I like your shirt."

"Thanks," she says, and gives me a thumbs-up.

I sit down at my desk and take out my math journal. I open it to the latest math journal investigation.

I used the formula to draw the cube. It's easy. You draw a square. Then you put your pencil in the center of that square to start another square. Then you draw diagonal lines to connect the corners of one square to the corners of the other. *Voilà*. Perfect cube every time.

But I guess I can work on it a little more, add some shading, try to get more of the three dimensions.

"Who measured what?" Mr. Vann asks when he appears at the door at exactly seven minutes after one. He goes to his desk and starts rummaging through the top drawer. He takes out a flashlight, turns it on and off a few times, and puts it back.

Chelsea raises her hand.

"I used inches to measure the length of my notebook," she says very clearly. "It is actually eleven inches long." She holds up her notebook for everyone to see. "Actually, we did the same thing in fourth grade. My mom is actually concerned that this question was too easy."

Mr. Vann often says why use a boring word when you can use a scintillating word? Chelsea seems to think that this means she should use the word *actually* as much as possible.

"I agree." Mr. Vann nods. "But why not start with the easy questions? The difficult ones will be along soon enough."

Mr. Vann wanders around the room as other kids share their journal entries.

"I used light-years to measure the distance to supernova SN 2014J," Dee Dee shares. "Distance—eleven million five hundred thousand light-years, give or take."

Mr. Vann stops behind me. I wonder if he's looking over my shoulder and seeing what I drew. I wonder if he knows what it is.

When I get home from school, Mom is in her room lying down. No one talks about how the peach feels after they cut the bad spot out.

"You okay?" I ask from the doorway.

"Just a little sore," she assures me. "Plus, I need to rest up for trick-or-treating."

Now is probably not the time to tell her that I'm getting a little old for trick-or-treating with my mom. I was hoping maybe Ella and I could go by ourselves this year.

Mom pats the side of the bed. I walk over and carefully sit down. I don't want to bump her. Then the phone rings.

I can tell it's my dad, which is kind of weird. It's not like my mom and dad hate each other, but it's not like they talk on the phone every day, either.

Once when I asked Mom why she and my dad got divorced (after she assured me that "the decision was set in motion long before I was on the scene"), she said that they just didn't have that much to talk about. But today, it seems like they have tons to talk about. My dad's a doctor, and he loves to talk about doctor stuff.

Mom starts asking him a list of questions. I don't understand much of it, but it sounds like the doctors want to do some kind of test. Then I hear Mom say a word that I don't know.

I raise my hand like I'm at school trying to ask a question. But Mom just holds up a finger, which is code for "Please wait, Mika. I'm on the phone."

I get up and go to my mom's office to use her laptop. If she asks, I'll tell her it's for homework.

Melanoma. That's the word I heard her say to my dad. That's the name of the thing they found in the spot on her leg. I say it out loud a few times. It sounds spooky.

When I Google it, a ton of websites come up—Wikipedia and Cancer.org and some place called the Mayo Clinic. That would be funny if things weren't suddenly so definitely unfunny right now. (I mean, why do they need a whole clinic just for mayonnaise?)

There's so much information on the screen, I don't even know where to start. I read through the short descriptions next to each web address. Some of the sentences are super science-y and complicated. I wish I had

Dee Dee here. She would probably understand a lot more than I do.

But some of the sentences are clear enough. Melanoma is the most dangerous form of skin cancer. Melanoma is life-threatening. Every hour, one person dies from it.

I shut the laptop. I don't even "save and sleep" like I'm supposed to.

This is not the kind of math I want to think about. This is really not the kind of thing I want to measure.

Math Journal Entry #6: Multiple Personalities

Measure something, anything. Then give at least three alternate but equal measurements for that object. For example, Mr. Vann is 6 feet tall. Mr. Vann is 2 yards tall. Mr. Vann is 72 inches tall. Mr. Vann is approximately 1/1000 of a mile tall.

Explain your thinking using words, numbers, and/or pictures.

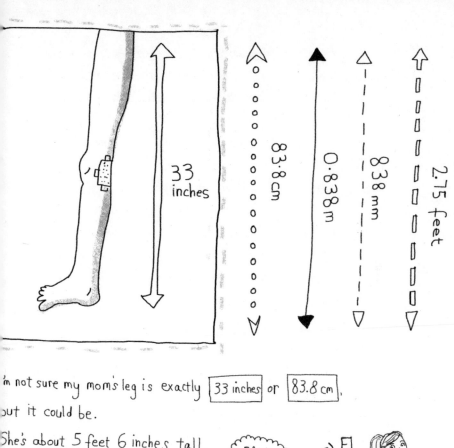

33 inches

83.8 cm

0.838 m

838 mm

2.75 feet

I'm not sure my mom's leg is exactly 33 inches or 83.8 cm, but it could be.

She's about 5 feet 6 inches tall, and in science we learned that your legs make up approximately half your height,

5 feet 6 inches

half of my height

so this is mostly estimation.

"One light-year is the same as five-point-eight tril-lion miles," Dee Dee reads from her math journal. She's dressed up as a Jedi from *Star Wars*. "That's the same as nine-point-four-six trillion kilometers."

"Twelve hundred bonus points for Dee Dee!" Mr. Vann shouts.

Today, Mr. Vann is *actually* wearing a cape and a top hat. He's also carrying a pumpkin under his arm. The pumpkin has a silly face drawn on it with permanent marker. Whenever Mr. Vann goes to write something on the board, he has to put the pumpkin down. Then two minutes later, he can't remember where he put it.

"I've lost my head!" he shouts for about the twenti-eth time.

"What are you supposed to be, anyway?" Dan asks. "The headless horseman?"

"Oh, no," Mr. Vann says. "I am the mindless student."

Dan is (surprise, surprise) a baseball player. At lunch he challenged Dee Dee to a duel—plastic light saber versus plastic baseball bat. Principal Mir quickly confis-cated both.

I saw Ella across the cafeteria during the duel. She was with the Onesies. They had matching T-shirts and oversized-pacifier necklaces. I guess she'll be trick-or-treating with them. Maybe I could ask Dee Dee what she's doing. Or maybe I'll just skip it this year.

"Are light-years going to be on the chapter test?" Chelsea raises her scepter to ask the question. (She's dressed as a princess.) "Because light-years are not in the textbook. And *actually,* the fifth-grade math standard for measurement only goes up to miles."

Mr. Vann just looks around and shouts, "I've lost my head!"

I didn't dress up today. Usually I put a lot of time and thought into my Halloween costume. Last year, I was Monet's Domino. I had a black rectangular sandwich board with six circles on each side. But instead of the circles being white, I painted a section of Monet's *Water Lilies* in each one.

I want to see the real *Water Lilies* in Paris so badly. But it's eight huge paintings that are way too big to move, so it's not like they're coming to the museum in Utica anytime soon. Mom says we'll go to Paris when I graduate from high school, which might as well be in a million light-years.

This year, I was planning to be a Monet Rubik's Cube. Same idea, but a little more complicated. I was going to get a big box and paint it black. Then I was going to copy four paintings from *Water Lilies*—one for each side of the cube. I know a cube has six sides, but I wasn't going to worry about the top and bottom. No one would see them anyway.

Then I was going to cut each of the paintings into nine equal squares and glue the squares onto the box, but all out of order. So if you could move the squares (which you can't because it's really just a big box with suspenders), you could try to get each painting back to normal.

But I haven't even started working on my costume. I haven't carved a jack-o'-lantern or found the corny old CD of spooky sound effects Mom keeps in the holiday box in the basement. I just don't feel like pretending to be scared.

Unit 4

Place Value

Today, Mr. Vann begins class by announcing that Chelsea was correct.

"You, dear thinkers, are *actually* being challenged too much," he tells us sympathetically.

Everybody knows that Chelsea said exactly the opposite, but we're not about to tell Mr. Vann that we want him to make our work even *harder*.

"So we are traveling further back into the future," Mr. Vann says. "All the way back to chapter three."

I think about this idea of going back to the future. If we're going *back* to it, I guess it means we've been there before, so we already know what's going to happen.

But I'm not so interested in going back to the future. I think I'd rather just go back to the past. Probably third grade. I really liked my third-grade teacher, and we had an art club after school and went on a field trip to this cool living history museum. My mom came as a parent helper.

Mr. Vann starts erasing the board with his right hand and writing the longest number I think I've ever seen with his left. Then he goes back from right to left, adding a decimal point and several commas.

"Who would care to read?" he says with one eyebrow raised.

Dan starts reading off the numbers on the board, but he reads them like they're in a list, not like they're making up a larger number.

"Partial credit," Mr. Vann responds. "I am certainly glad that you recognize all the symbols I have written on the board." Everybody laughs.

Dee Dee raises her hand and reads off the number— three hundred twenty-seven trillion and something hundredths. Then she tells us what the number would be in scientific notation.

Mr. Vann gives her three hundred twenty-seven trillion and something hundredths bonus points.

"If it's scientific notation," Dan mutters, "we should be learning about it in science."

I guess Dan hasn't figured out how mixed up fifth grade at the middle school can be.

"I will raise the issue with the science department," Mr. Vann says. "But for now, dear thinkers, please name some things that require very large numbers in order to be described." He starts pacing in front of the board. "Come on," he says. "Shout 'em out."

I won't bother mentioning that teachers are usually telling kids to *stop* shouting out. Mr. Vann often encourages it.

"The number of fairies on the head of a pin," Chelsea offers.

"Possibly." Mr. Vann nods.

"The number of people living on the continent of Asia," a girl named Olivia says.

"The Yankees' total payroll!" Dan shouts.

"The number of neutrons in all of the atoms in the human body," Dee Dee says with a smile.

Dee Dee likes to say things that only she and Mr. Vann will understand. It usually gets her a bunch of bonus points. Today, her T-shirt has a copy of the periodic table of elements on the front. On the back, it says: *I wear this shirt periodically.*

"The total number of notebooks in Highbridge Middle School," Chelsea tries.

Again with the notebooks. But *actually,* if you estimate three hundred kids per grade times four grades, that's 1,200 kids. Even if every kid has five notebooks, that's still only 6,000 notebooks, which isn't *that* big a number.

Now everybody is shouting, and it's really, really loud. I notice Principal Mir in the hall. She pokes her head in the doorway.

Principal Mir likes to walk around the building with a tiny notepad in one hand and a tiny pencil in the other. When she's not writing things down, she keeps the pencil behind her ear.

But Mr. Vann doesn't see Principal Mir because he's walking around the room with his eyes closed again, waving his arms like an orchestra conductor. He holds a dry-erase marker like a baton. He listens closely to certain sections of the room and then moves on. He gestures for some kids to shout louder, and other kids to shout softer.

"The number of calories in ten Big Macs!"

"The number of miles on Mr. Vann's car!"

"The number of rats living in the basement of High-bridge Middle!"

I figure it's so loud, I might as well say what's on my mind. Maybe it will feel good. Maybe I'll feel better if I just say the words out loud.

"The number of people every year who get . . ."

Of course, Mr. Vann hushes everyone just as I say "skin cancer" really loud.

"Very true," Mr. Vann says. He gives me a nod and three million bonus points.

I can't help smiling a little. I mean, that's a lot of bonus points.

I barely get home before I have to get into the car. At least this time, Mom had the appointment on the to-do list. She's going to the medical center to have the test that she and my dad were talking about. It's supposed to tell us something, something important, I guess.

"Jeannie will meet us there and drive us home," Mom says as she pulls out of the driveway. "I might be a little loopy." She makes a silly face.

I don't bother with "I know you're loopy, but what am I?" I just don't feel like it.

"My first tattoo," she says in her Mom-trying-to-be-cool way. As part of this procedure, they have to inject some kind of ink into my mom's leg. I know she's just trying to lighten things up, but my mom is like the *last* person on earth who would ever get a tattoo.

"We're lucky we have such a great medical center so close by," she says as we pull into the parking garage.

I'm thinking we'd be luckier if we didn't have to go at all.

When they take Mom in for the procedure, I stay in the waiting room and do my homework. Then I half pay attention to this silly game show that's on TV. There are lots of lights and colors and sound effects. Everybody on the show is so excited. They are so ridiculously happy.

I take my oil pastels and a blank book out of my backpack. I'm not really drawing anything, just lines and dots and scribbles.

After a while, a nurse comes through the door and

looks around. "Mika Barnes?" she asks in my direction. I raise my hand like I'm at school.

"Hi, I'm Ana," she says. "Your mom's doing great. I'm supposed to tell you that Jeannie's running a bit late, but she's on her way."

I'm not surprised. Jeannie is often "running a bit late."

"Thanks," I say. But instead of leaving, the nurse sits down on the waiting room couch next to me.

"This show is so weird." She nods up toward the TV. "So how are you?"

I shrug. I don't really have an answer. I guess I'm okay. I'm not the one who's sick, right?

"Do you have any questions?" she asks next.

I think for a minute. Lately, it seems like whenever I ask Mom a question, she just tells me there's nothing for me to worry about. She doesn't say there's *nothing* to worry about, just that there's nothing for *me* to worry about.

Or she does that grown-up sneaky strategy of choosing her words very carefully. Like when I was little and I asked her if Santa was real. She said, "Santa Claus is the spirit of Christmas, which is very real." So not a lie, but not the straight truth, either.

"Anything you want to know?" Ana tries again.

I think about what I want to know. But I don't know if I really want to know what I want to know. But the not-knowing is like this loud echo in my head. And I remember what Mr. Vann says—it's always better to know.

I start with an easy question. "What's the ink for?" I ask.

"You see, cancer cells can travel," Ana explains.

Figures. Travel is supposed to be a good thing, like going on a cruise or a safari or going to Paris after your high school graduation. But I can tell from the look on Ana's face that this kind of travel is not good.

"They can travel through the lymphatic system," she continues. "Think of it like a bunch of highways going all over your body. Your lymph nodes are like the tollbooths along the way. The doctors inject the ink to see which tollbooth the cancer would get to first. Then they look at *that* node, the sentinel node, under the microscope. Best case scenario, it's clean." Ana smiles.

I suddenly get this weird picture in my mind of a super-clean tollbooth, all sparkly and shiny. Maybe those fifth-grade aliens who came down from space to find their home pods made it their mission to scrub that tollbooth like nobody's business.

Ana gives my knee a squeeze. "And if it's clean," she says, "chances are we caught it in time."

Math Journal Entry #7

Write a number that represents something, anything.

Your number should span the hundred-thousands place all the way to the hundredths place.

First, "dissect" your number. Explain which digit is in which place, and the value that each digit represents.

Then have fun "playing" with your number. In other words, move that decimal point and see what happens!

Famous TV and commercial personality

Jeannie Katigbak

earned a total of one hundred twenty one
thousand, seven hundred and eighty-one
dollars and fifty-six hundredths of a
dollar (or cents) last year.

Let's say Jeannie donated twenty thousand dollars to Highbridge Middle School marching tuba and jug band.

That would change the 2 in the ten thousands place to a 0, and she would only have $101,781.56 left.

But now let's imagine Jeannie loses her recurring role on the popular soap opera "As the World Squirms" and makes a less-than-wise investment in a new line of hamster toothpaste. This causes the decimal point in her salary to move a full five spaces to the left. Jeannie would be reduced to a mere one dollar and one point seven, eight, one, five, six cents.

That's two cents (if you estimate).

Maybe I shouldn't have used Jeannie for the latest math journal conundrum. But it was super fun drawing her and her hamster toothpaste.

Jeannie's not exactly famous, but she is the kind of actress you see on TV a lot if you know to look for her. Last year she did this commercial for car insurance that was on *all* the time. She jokes that one commercial bought her a new car, and Jeannie has a really nice car.

Jeannie comes over for dinner a lot when she's not out of town for work. She just shows up. Then Mom's line is, "Would it kill you to call first?" But she doesn't really mean it.

I like it when Jeannie comes over. Sometimes "just the two of us" can get a little boring, and Jeannie's good at filling in the empty spaces.

"So, I spoke to a friend of a friend of a friend," Jeannie tells us excitedly as she unpacks the takeout. She holds up a container of some green-bean-salad thing. "Doesn't this look amazing?" she asks. "Almonds! I couldn't resist. Anyway, this person said that if they find something in your sen— What do you call it?"

"Sentinel node," I say.

Mom looks at me. She seems surprised that I know the answer.

"Right," Jeannie says. "That thing. Anyway, if they find something, they call you lickety-split because, you know, it's not . . . so good. But if they don't find anything, then they don't care about you as much anymore. No offense," she says in Mom's direction.

"None taken," Mom says.

"Then you get put in the 'this call can wait until later' pile. So if you haven't heard anything yet, you're totally in the clear."

Jeannie can be very convincing. I know she's not a doctor, even if she has played one on TV like a million times.

After the procedure last week, the *real* doctor said Mom's sentinel node appeared to be clean, but they would still need to send samples for more thorough testing, just to be 100 percent sure.

"I guess no news is good news," Mom says as she grabs three forks from the drawer.

I know what she means. She means that getting "no news" is equal to getting "good news." If I had to express it as a math equation:

No News = Good News.

But I can't help thinking about it the other way, too. It could also mean that there *actually* is no good news. Except right now there isn't any news, and according to Jeannie, that *is* good news. No news also means that you can just forget about all of it for a little while.

"Hi, Mika." Chelsea comes over to where I'm sitting by myself in the cafeteria. I'd hoped to sit with Ella, but by the time I got through the lunch line, she and the Onesies had already left.

Chelsea lowers her tray and sits down next to me. "You know, Mika, skin cancer isn't that serious. I mean, it's not like brain cancer or"—she looks around and hides her mouth behind her hand—"breast cancer. When you said that in math the other day, you seemed really worried. But you won't get it if you're careful. You just need to wear sunscreen and a hat. Like how you won't get lung cancer if you don't smoke."

"Actually . . . ," Dee Dee interrupts. She walks around to the other side of the table and plops her tray down. "Approximately ten percent of men and twenty percent of women who get lung cancer are nonsmokers."

Chelsea shrugs. I feel a little bad because I know she's just trying to be nice, but I'm not going to let it spoil my good day. There's still no news. And no news probably does mean good news.

This is all over, and my mom is fine, and now I can use my math journal for other things, like estimating the number of fairies on the head of a pin (thank you, Chelsea, for the idea), or recording the number of millimeters in a millipede's feet (using scientific notation, of course), or figuring out the amount of time that will elapse before we have to leave for math (exactly sixteen minutes).

"My mom's cousin's husband had lung cancer," Dan chimes in. He's on his way to bus his tray. "And he totally smoked."

Chelsea gives me a look that politely says I-told-you-so.

"Or maybe it was stomach cancer," Dan says. "But he still smoked."

"A lot of people think of cancer as an immune issue," Dee Dee says, cracking open her milk. "It has to do with how well your body can fight stuff. So smoking would still affect the quality of his overall health."

"What are you, a doctor?" Dan says sarcastically.

"Not yet." Dee Dee smiles. Today's T-shirt has a big picture of an arm bone. Underneath it, it says: *I found this humerus.*

I turn around and look up at Dan. "How's your mom's cousin's husband?" I ask. "Is he okay?"

"Oh, no," Dan says, heading for the garbage cans. "He totally croaked."

Right after I get home from school, the phone rings.

Like finding things and traveling, phone ringing is usually a good thing. If it's not someone calling my mom for work, it's usually Jeannie or Ella, although Ella hasn't called in a while. But now that I think about it, I guess I haven't tried calling her, either.

Or else it's Grandma Beau. That's my mom's mom. Grandma Beau just lives over in Schenectady, but she still calls every day.

I hear Mom pick up the phone in her office, but I don't hear her say "Hey there, Jeannie" or "Hi, Mom" or even "Rebecca Barnes and Associates." All I hear is nothing.

Then she finally says, "Yes, I do have family in the area." And then she says, "Yes, I'll expect their call." And then she hangs up.

I hear her pick up the phone again. It sounds like she's leaving a message. She hangs up, picks up, and dials again. I can't hear exactly what she's saying, but it sounds like she's saying the same thing every time.

After a few minutes, the phone rings. Mom picks it up, and I hear her say, "Oh, Hugh." It's my dad, and the way she says his name sounds like someone letting the air out of a balloon all at once.

I can't understand what they're saying because my mom is in the other room. Plus, she's talking really fast. Then she hangs up the phone, and it immediately rings again.

"Mommy?" I hear her say.

Now I'm really confused. *She's* Mommy. Then I realize it must be Grandma Beau.

When my mom finally comes out of her office, about twenty-one million phone calls later, her eyes are red and her face is all puffy.

"It's okay, Mika-Mouse," she says to me. "It's going to be okay."

She goes to the fridge and opens the door. She stares into the fridge for a long time before she asks, "What should we do for dinner? It's just the two of us tonight. Just the girls."

What she doesn't say is what I somehow already know. The tollbooth wasn't clean after all.

Math Journal Entry #8: Scratch and Match

Divide your page into three columns. (Those are the ones that go up and down, Dan.)

In the left column, list four numbers.

In the center column, write those numbers in expanded form. (Please remember to attend to precision.)

In the right column, list the things those numbers enumerate.

Be sure to scramble the order of your lists! Someone else will have to match them up.

Scratch and Match

1,236.8	10 zillion + 7 zillion	number of fairies on the head of a pin
87,000	$1,000 + 200 + 30 + 6 + 0.8$	distance (in miles) from Albany International Airport to Orlando International Airport
17 zillion	$(20 + 1)$ million	people in the US who will be diagnosed with melanoma this year
21 million	$80,000 + 7,000$	number of times the phone rang yesterday

Scratch and Match is *actually* the name of a lottery game where you scratch off the silver stuff with a coin. If you have three numbers that match, you win that amount of money. Rumor has it Mr. Vann won ten thousand dollars once. That's a one in the ten-thousands place and a whole mess of zeroes.

I guess Mr. Vann is lucky like that. I wonder what the odds are of winning ten thousand dollars. I wonder if it's more or less than the odds of getting cancer.

"Dear thinkers," Mr. Vann announces, "please partner up."

Dee Dee looks over at me with a little shrug. I pick up my math journal and bring it to her desk. Her T-shirt today simply says: *This is what a scientist looks like.*

"Now," Mr. Vann says once everyone is settled, "switch journals with your partner. You are going to use deductive reasoning and good old common sense to match each number with its expanded form, as well as the concept that both enumerate. And remember," Mr. Vann warns, "no peeking at your partner's other pages. Except for this page, math journals are the private property of the math journalist."

I guess Mr. Vann is the only one who's allowed to peek.

I look over Dee Dee's lists. All of her numbers have to do with different kinds of science stuff. I draw a tentative line between "the closest the Earth gets to Jupiter" and "390,682,810 miles."

"You probably should have been partners with Chelsea," Dee Dee says as she looks over my list. "But you're in luck. She told me just yesterday that there are, in fact, exactly seventeen zillion fairies on the head of a pin. So that one's easy. The rest I have no clue about."

"Put on your thinking caps!" Mr. Vann yells as he walks around the room.

"I knew I forgot something this morning." Dee Dee sighs and pats her head. "Let's see, I also happen to know that your phone rang precisely twenty-one million times yesterday." She draws a thick line between the words and the numbers.

"I know this because my sister obviously went over to *your* house due to the fact that she managed to get her phone taken away at *my* house on account of completely unacceptable overage charges." Dee Dee is funny even when you don't feel like laughing.

"And I'm going to guess that one thousand, two hundred, and whatever goes with the distance, in miles, from Albany International Airport—airport code ALB, by the way—to Orlando International Airport, airport code MCO on account of its original name: McCoy Air Force Base," she says matter-of-factly. "What's in Orlando? I mean, besides Mickey Mouse."

"My dad," I say.

"Lucky you," she says.

"I guess," I say.

"Melanoma?" Dee Dee says next. "Yuckety yuck yuck

yuck. I'm going to match that with eighty-seven thousand because it sounds like something you actually looked up, and eighty-seven thousand is the only real number left."

Mr. Vann happens to be passing by just as Dee Dee says that. "Real numbers will be addressed in chapter two, dear Dee Dee," he says. "Let's not get ahead of ourselves. Or should I say, as we are currently at chapter three, let's not get behind ourselves."

Dee Dee rolls her eyes. I smile. Mr. Vann gives everyone a five-minute warning.

"So how did I do?" Dee Dee asks.

I write a *100%* at the top of the page, with smiley faces in the zeroes. Then I write *RM* in big bubble letters.

"What's RM?" she asks.

"Refrigerator Material," I say. "My mom writes that. But I guess since it's in my math journal, you can't put it on your fridge. Sorry."

"No sweat," Dee Dee says. She looks over the page in her math journal and gives me a 100 percent, too. "Why melanoma?" she asks.

I haven't told anyone at school about my mom, not even Ella. Every time I see her, she's surrounded by Onesies. We just wave in the halls.

But Dee Dee knows a lot about all kinds of science stuff. Plus, she's smart and funny and nice. I wait approximately seven seconds of elapsed time. Then I tell her.

Unit 5

Real and Rational Numbers

"Mika and Dee Dee have expressed a real interest in real numbers," Mr. Vann announces from the door.

It's been a few days since Dee Dee said *real numbers,* and she didn't even mean it in a math way.

"So we are moving further back in time," Mr. Vann says mysteriously, "all the way back to chapter two."

I can't help noticing that Mr. Vann has appeared in the doorway four minutes early, and since it's sleeting outside and everybody's already here, today math starts at 1:03. If this were a normal class, kids would moan and groan, but nobody does.

Mr. Vann writes on the board: Real numbers can be positive or negative. Real numbers are not imaginary numbers.

I'm waiting to hear what Dan has to say about imaginary

numbers. Any minute now I expect him to start counting: *goop, cheen, bloopy-boo.*

But Dan is absent. And he's not the only one. There are only two days of school this week, then Thanksgiving break. Now I remember Dan saying that he was going to Cleveland to see his grandparents.

"Let's talk about zero," Mr. Vann says. "Is zero real?"

"Is anything real?" a kid named Kevin asks back. He seems to be filling in for Dan as resident smart aleck today.

"Interesting point," Mr. Vann says. "But let's limit the conversation to math, or else we'll just . . ." Mr. Vann hooks his thumbs together to make a bird or a butterfly. Then he flaps his fingers into flight.

"Zero has not always been on the world stage," Mr. Vann continues. "Many ancient civilizations had no concept of zero."

"Zero is nothing," Chelsea chimes in.

Mr. Vann raises his eyebrows in encouragement, but Chelsea doesn't seem to have anything more to say.

"And nothing is *something,*" Dee Dee helps her out. "It *is* a value. So zero is real."

"Right," Chelsea adds. "Because zero is nothing, it is *actually* something."

"Five trillion bonus points for the both of you," Mr. Vann says with a smile.

And mixed up as it is, I totally understand what Dee Dee and Chelsea mean. Even nothing is something. Like if the doctors find nothing in your sentinel node, that's something—something good.

"Please find a real partner with whom to create a real number line for your real numbers," Mr. Vann tells us. He hands Dee Dee a stack of long strips of paper. "And remember," he says, "your number line should feature zero, our newfound hero."

"You mean *she*-ro," Dee Dee says as she starts passing out the paper strips. "One to a customer!" she shouts.

"Well, technically, one to every half a customer, as we're working in pairs," Mr. Vann mutters. "But as fractions won't be covered until chapter nine . . ."

Chelsea hurries over to my desk. "I don't know about you," she whispers, "but I don't think we should be starting a new unit right before Thanksgiving."

"Probably not," I say. I don't really care, but I don't feel much like talking.

"Also," Chelsea continues, "you can't define a word with its opposite. You can't say that real numbers are *not* imaginary numbers. My mom is going to speak to Principal Mir. My mom's on the school board, you know. She thinks Mr. Vann *actually* belongs in an alternative school, not Highbridge Middle."

"Your mom must have a lot of time on her hands," I say quietly. I don't know if I want Chelsea to hear me or not, but she doesn't seem to. She's fishing around in her backpack for something.

Chelsea comes up for air and hands me a ruler. "You draw, Mika," she says. "You're the artist, after all."

I spread the strip of paper out on my desk. The ends droop over the sides. I draw a dash in the middle and label it with a big, fat zero. Then I draw a silly face inside it. Chelsea smiles.

"But shouldn't the zero be over here?" she asks, pointing to the left. "I mean, so we have somewhere to go."

"We need to leave room for the negative numbers," I say.

"Oh, right," Chelsea says. "I guess I don't like to be negative," she adds with a little giggle.

"Think like a proton," I can't help joking.

On the way home from the bus, I open up my first trimester progress report.

It's not like you get real grades on your progress report. Each teacher just writes a few sentences to let people know how you're doing. Some teachers copy and paste the same thing for everybody. Like my language arts comment says: *Fifth graders are reading dramas on the theme of early North American life.* I'm pretty sure everybody got that one.

For art, it looks like Mrs. Poole copied and pasted: *Work: Satisfactory. Effort: Satisfactory.* But then she checked the box: *Seems distracted at times.* I feel a little prick at the back of my eyes. I've never gotten a negative comment in art before.

And negative is a bad thing, except, of course, with cancer. With cancer, negative is a good thing. Like when they looked at my mom's tattooed lymph node more thoroughly, it would have been great if it was negative.

And positive is supposed to a good thing. Like a positive attitude, which my mom is always talking about. "Good energy is contagious" is her new go-to line on that topic. This weekend she scrubbed the house from top to bottom, and then she rearranged the furniture in the living room about twenty times before ending up with it the same way it's always been.

I look back at my progress report. Mr. Vann has gone outside the lines of the math section. I read: Mika shows exceptional attention, effort, and participation in math. She carefully, thoughtfully, and creatively shares her thinking, using her talent in the visual arts to help communicate complex math concepts. Grade Five Pod Two Math Block C is lucky to have her.

I suddenly get this picture in my mind of a life-size number line that you could *actually* walk on. And I know that if I plotted Mrs. Poole's negative comment to the left of zero, and Mr. Vann's positive comment to the right of zero, Mr. Vann would be much further away, which is a good thing.

When I walk in the door, Mom is sitting at the kitchen table. She looks like she's been waiting for me. I'm a little surprised that she remembered it was progress report day. But it's the kind of thing she would have written on the calendar back at the beginning of the school year. She pulls out a chair for me to sit down next to her.

I hand her the envelope. She looks at it for a second, and then sets it down without even taking the progress report out. If I had to comment on her reading, I would also check: *Seems distracted at times.*

"So, Mika-Mouse," Mom starts. I suddenly realize we're not here to look over my progress report. We're here for another big explanation.

"It looks like it's going to take a little longer to deal with all this." She pauses.

I really wish she would define *longer*. If the whole purpose of measurement is to get a handle on things, exactly how much time are we talking about?

"The good news is they only found a very small something," she continues. "The next step is that they'll need to remove a few more lymph nodes, just to make sure."

Mom has laid out the plan, but I'm still confused. "I thought no news was good news," I manage.

"Well, it seems there was a delay getting the lab results, what with Veterans Day being a holiday and all." She says this as if it's no big deal, like we're talking about the mail coming late or something.

"Is Jeannie taking you?" I ask. I'm wondering if this appointment means more early-morning-home-alone time for me. Or if it's an after-school thing, and it means more stuck-in-the-waiting-room-watching-ridiculous-game-shows time.

"Actually," Mom says, "I'll have to stay in the hospital for a couple of days. So Grandma Beau is coming. She was coming for Thanksgiving anyway, so . . ." Her voice trails off.

I get that weird feeling at the back of my neck again, like someone is squeezing it even though no one is. "So it's an *operation*," I say.

"Well, that's one word for it," Mom says.

Grandma Beau doesn't stay overnight very often. First of all, she lives pretty close. Plus, the only place for her to sleep is the futon couch in Mom's office. Our house is fine for the two of us, but it's pretty small. "Buy the least expensive house in the nicest neighborhood in the best school district." That's one of Mom's rules of advice for her clients.

Another rule is not to buy stuff that you don't really need. Grandma Beau, on the other hand, spends a lot of time buying things at estate sales and then reselling them online. Whenever she comes over, she brings her "big box of treasures" for me to help her sort through. Mom calls it her "big box of other people's garbage." But I love looking through the jewelry and postcards and figurines. Last time, I found this tiny ceramic moose. It's standing guard on my desk.

I hear a car pull up and look out the window. It's Grandma Beau.

"She's here *now*?" I say. I feel like I'm watching a movie where I've missed the first half hour and I have no idea what's going on.

"Well, your dad made a few calls, and there happened to be a cancellation, and because it's a holiday week, they didn't want to get too far behind in the timeline," Mom says. I understand all the words she's saying, but the sentences make absolutely no sense.

Grandma Beau comes in the front door, carrying two suitcases. She drops the bigger one on the floor and hands the smaller one to my mom.

"Everybody needs a decent bag," Grandma Beau says. Grandma Beau always seems to know when you need something that you don't even know you need. "We're just lucky they could squeeze you in tomorrow."

We'd be even luckier if they didn't have to squeeze her in at all, I think. But I don't say it out loud. Instead, I ask, "Where's your box of treasures?"

Grandma Beau just waves her hands around and shrugs her shoulders. Like maybe she forgot it, or maybe she decided not to bring it, or maybe treasures are for people who don't have to be at the hospital the next day.

"Let me make sure I've got the plan," Grandma Beau says as she sits down at the table with a sigh. "First, we drop you off." She nods toward my mom. "We'll get you settled. Then Mika and I will get some breakfast. At seven-forty, I drop Mika at school. Then I'll come back to you." She nods at Mom again. "At two-forty, I pick

77

Mika up from school, and we'll both come back. Do I have it?"

Mom nods.

"Why can't I just stay at the hospital with Grandma Beau?" I ask.

"Absolutely not," Mom says. "It's a school day."

"But it's the day before a vacation," I say. "I mean, Dan P.'s already in Cleveland."

Mom just looks at me confused and asks if I've done my homework.

Math Journal Entry #9

Think about some real numbers in real life.

Then express yourself in a mathematical expression!

I used to sing this song when I was little: *What comes after one? Two comes after one. What comes after two? Three comes after two. What comes after three?* You get the idea. Mom says I used to sing that song for hours.

I don't know why I liked that song so much back then, but I know why I like it now. It tells you exactly what is coming down the line, and the next thing is always just another friendly, goofy-looking number.

That's what the picture in my math journal is supposed to be, although I guess I forgot to explain it.

Mr. Vann stops for a long time to peek over my shoulder. I'm waiting for him to point out that my expression isn't complete. It has numbers but no symbols, no operators.

Instead, he hands me a sticky note worth ten million bonus points.

According to my calculations, I now have 14,500,011 bonus points. Too bad they're not real.

After Grandma Beau picks me up from school, according to Mom's plan, we head back to the hospital.

"She's in recovery and everything went very well," Grandma Beau tells me. Then she turns her attention to the GPS to follow the directions.

As Grandma Beau drives, I start playing a game in my head. I make up new rules for the trip. Like, if I see at least three red cars before we get to the hospital, everything will be okay. Or if there are more than two dogs between here and the next red light, everything will be fine.

We end up in a different waiting room this time, but it has the same couches and the same stupid game show on the TV. Grandma Beau goes to the vending machines and brings back snacks Mom would never let me get. The colors seem too bright in the gray room—orange chips and red candy and purple soda.

After what feels like a very long stretch of elapsed time, a doctor-looking woman comes in to speak with Grandma Beau. They whisper in a corner. I see Grandma Beau nodding. Then she takes out a little notebook and starts writing things down.

"Well, it's not the best news," Grandma Beau says when she finally comes. "But it's not the worst news. It's kind of like the best-worst news, or maybe it's the worst-best news."

"I don't get it," I say.

"They found a tiny something in one node," Grandma Beau reads from her notes. "And the doctor says that one is better than two. Two is better than three, and three is *much* better than four. More than four is . . ." Grandma Beau stops talking.

And once again, everything is completely mixed up. Usually you want bigger numbers, like when you're a little kid and you can't wait for your next birthday. When I turned ten last year, I thought double digits was such a big deal.

Or if you buy a lottery ticket, you want the prize to be really huge, with place values all the way to the millions. Not that Mom would ever let me buy a lottery ticket. "Don't spend real money on unreal chances." That's another one of her rules.

But with cancer, big numbers are bad, even big numbers as small as four. There's nothing in the hundreds place. Nothing in the tens place, even. But a four in the ones place is a big, bad number.

"I still don't get it," I say, more to myself than Grandma Beau.

"If they find something in four or more nodes"— Grandma Beau looks down at her little notebook—"it statistically increases the likelihood that the cancer has traveled elsewhere."

And like we know, travel is not a good thing.

"No matter," Grandma Beau says, closing her notebook. "We've only got the one to worry about."

I don't point out that this node is in addition to the sentinel node. To express it as a mathematical expression:

$$1 + 1 = 2.$$

But I guess two isn't that bad. It's not as bad as three, which isn't as bad as four. It's just not as good as one. And none of them are what I really wished for, which was just plain zero.

We spend Thanksgiving Day with my mom in the hospital. Mostly, we watch the parade on TV. Jeannie brings us fancy turkey sandwiches overflowing with avocado and sprouts and stuff.

Grandma Beau's phone keeps dinging and pinging with different messages, probably about her latest round of treasures. At one point, her phone actually rings. She looks at the screen and hands it to me.

"Your father," she says.

"Welcome to holidays in the hospital," Dad says with a little chuckle. I don't know if that's supposed to be funny. It's hard to hear him because of all the background noise. He's obviously at work. "How are you, Mika?" he asks.

I want to say, "How do you think I am? It's Thanksgiving and I'm sitting in a plastic chair eating stale potato chips." But all I say is, "I'm okay."

"How's your mom?" he asks next.

I don't really have an answer to that question, either. I assume he knows she's in a hospital bed with her leg propped up and a bunch of tubes going everywhere.

"They say she can go home tomorrow," I tell him.

"That's fantastic," Dad says way too enthusiastically. Then I hear some kind of intercom in the background. "Listen, Mika, sorry, but I've got to go. Happy Thanksgiving, honey."

"Happy—" I start, but he's already hung up.

When we get home on Friday, Grandma Beau sets Mom up on the couch with a blanket and a stack of pillows under her leg. I bring in my sleeping bag and put it on the floor in front of the TV. Grandma Beau pops some popcorn. It's cozy.

We watch a movie about aliens who dress up like human teenagers so they can go to high school. They look normal, but they don't know how to act, so they do ridiculous things, like eat the straws in the cafeteria. It's a terrible movie. But at least nobody in it gets sick.

The weird thing is I keep forgetting why I'm sitting on the floor eating popcorn. It's nice having Grandma Beau here and vegging out in front of the TV with no school and no homework. I keep thinking that we should do this for Thanksgiving every year. This should become our new tradition.

Then I turn around and see my mom on the couch and remember.

"Have we forgotten everything we learned before Turkey Day?" Mr. Vann asks on Monday. "Is all that tryptophan still making you sleepy? I ask you again, dear thinkers, what makes a number rational?"

Nobody knows the answer. Then suddenly, Mr. Vann seems to remember that we didn't get to rational numbers before the break. "Oh, right," he mumbles.

He writes on the board: Rational numbers are not irrational numbers.

Chelsea catches my eye and gives me a knowing look. Then she mouths, "You can't define a word with its opposite."

I'm waiting for Dan to come up with some joke about irrational numbers being totally nutso, but he's absent again. At this rate, he's probably going to miss the whole unit.

"The number three is a rational number," Mr. Vann begins. "Sixty-seven thousandths is a rational number. Pi is not a rational number. The square root of ninety-nine is not a rational number. Have we got it?"

Chelsea raises her hand. "I'm confused," she says.

I'm confused, too. Usually I don't mind hanging in there and trying to figure out Mr. Vann's riddles, but today, I'm tired. I just want someone to give us the answer. I flip to the end of the textbook to see if there's a glossary.

"Agreed." Mr. Vann nods to Chelsea. But instead of explaining, he continues with his list of examples. "The square root of two is irrational. That's not to say the square root of two is crazy." Mr. Vann chuckles at his own joke. "But rather, the square root of two cannot be expressed as a ratio of two integers."

"What's an integer again?" a girl named Lola calls from the back.

"Hmm," says Mr. Vann. "Probably should have led with that."

"And what's a square root?" Miles asks.

"Ratio?" Chelsea pleads.

"I see," Mr. Vann says. "It seems that we are going about this all out of order. But as order of operations won't be covered until chapter fourteen . . ."

Mr. Vann wanders around the room like he's not sure what to do next. When he gets to my desk, he leans down and says, "Mika, might I borrow your most recent math journal creation? It's your call. No pressure. Feel free to say no."

"Um, sure," I say.

I hand my math journal to Mr. Vann. He brings it up to the document projector and finds the right page. My dancing numbers pop up on the board in full color.

"Yay, Mika!" Chelsea whispers, and she does a few mini claps in front of her face.

"So cool," Dee Dee says. She gives me a thumbs-up.

"These, dear thinkers, are our integers." Mr. Vann points to each of the numbers in the line. "They are real, and they are rational."

Then Mr. Vann points to the space between my dancing two and dancing three. "Everything between them is also real. But alas, not all of it can be rational."

Math Journal Entry #10

Plot a number line,
So fabulous and fine,
Some rational, some real,
Then to really seal the deal,
Or just to be contrary,
Some even imaginary.

Explain your thinking using words, numbers, and/or pictures.

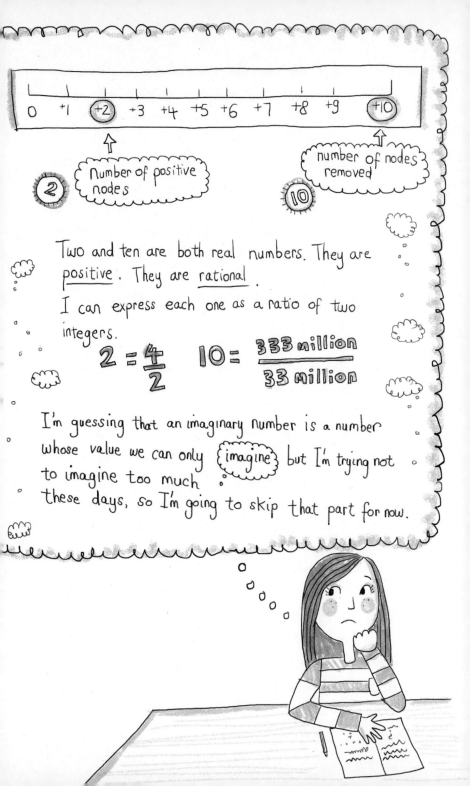

Number of positive nodes

2

number of nodes removed

10

Two and ten are both real numbers. They are positive. They are rational.

I can express each one as a ratio of two integers.

$$2 = \frac{4}{2} \qquad 10 = \frac{333\text{ million}}{33\text{ million}}$$

I'm guessing that an imaginary number is a number whose value we can only imagine but I'm trying not to imagine too much these days, so I'm going to skip that part for now.

Up until now, my mom didn't really seem sick. It was like something I knew in my head but couldn't see in real life. Everybody kept saying she had this terrible thing in her leg, so terrible that they had to cut it out, and then cut it out again. But at least Mom seemed pretty much the same, except for the big bandage on the back of her knee.

But now she has to keep her leg up all the time because it can get really, really swollen. Plus, she's silly one minute and totally out of it the next. It's like Rational Mom has suddenly been replaced by Irrational Mom.

"It's the pain medication," Grandma Beau says, as if this is supposed to explain everything.

I'm trying really hard to be helpful, to remember that "good energy is contagious," but Mom always calls for Grandma Beau to come help her. I think she doesn't want to scare me or gross me out.

She has this thing called a surgical drain. It's like a tiny straw coming right out of her hip that goes into this little plastic pouch. Grandma Beau says the drain is to catch the fluid that doesn't know where to go. Grandma Beau has to record how much fluid the bag collects every day, in milliliters.

"It's just until the other lymph nodes realize they have to pick up the slack," Grandma Beau tells me. "Until her body gets used to missing them."

I wonder if it's kind of like how Grandma Beau had to get used to missing Grandpa Beau. I know my Grandpa Beau got sick, and then he died. That happened before

I was even born. But I guess I used to think it was something that had always happened. Like it was always that way.

But now I see there was a time when it was *actually* happening, when everybody was in the middle of it, just like we're in the middle of this now.

I try to imagine the future, further down the number line. I've just graduated from high school, and Mom and I are on the plane to Paris.

"Remember that time you sprained your ankle in soccer?" she says.

"Remember the time the car broke down in that snowstorm?" I say.

"Oh, yeah, and remember that whole cancer thing?" I hear Mom saying as she ruffles my hair only once. "I'm sure glad that's behind us."

Then other times my mind starts skating out to this far-off place, and I try not to imagine if I could ever get used to missing Mom.

Unit 6

Equations and Inequalities

Today, Mr. Vann pops in the door seven minutes early. Everybody's already here, probably because the temperature outside has turned downright arctic lately.

"However challenging," Mr. Vann tells us for about the millionth time, "it is crucial to develop the habits of algebraic thinking."

But so far, algebraic thinking is a lot easier than it sounds. It's all about constants that stay the same, and variables that take something's place. Then the variables keep changing.

Algebraic thinking is Jeannie picking up our vacuum cleaner from the repair shop because Mom is taking a little longer to get back on her feet than expected, and she isn't cleared to drive yet.

Let *Jeannie* = *Mom*.

Algebraic thinking is Grandma Beau waking me up for school and making me breakfast because Mom had a hard night and has just fallen back to sleep an hour before I have to leave for the bus.

Let *Grandma Beau = Mom.*

Algebraic thinking is Mom giving a few clients to another accountant because it's still hard for her to sit for more than thirty minutes of elapsed time.

Let *Accountant #2 = Mom.*

"Remember," Mr. Vann says as he reaches into his desk drawer and pulls out a stack of sticky notes. "Always do unto the left side as you do unto the right. Let's see. Chelsea, please come up to the front, and Mika, please join her."

Chelsea and I walk to the front of the room. I shove my hands into my pockets. Chelsea just stands there, very straight.

Mr. Vann writes an x on a sticky note, pulls it off the stack, and sticks it on Chelsea's forehead. Then he does the same to me.

"Let's start with *two x equals eight,*" Mr. Vann explains. "Now we just need our eight."

He chooses eight kids to come to the front. Dee Dee's one of them. She walks slowly as if she's deep in thought, probably trying to solve some major puzzle of the universe. Today's T-shirt has a picture of the Milky Way with an arrow pointing to the center. At the end of the arrow, it says: *YOU ARE HERE.*

"So, if our dear Mika is an x," Mr. Vann says, "and our dear Chelsea is an x, how many of that pack of malcontents is each x entitled to?"

Mr. Vann points to the group of eight. Everybody's all slouchy and frowny, except for Dee Dee. She's bouncing from one foot to the other.

"Four!" Dan shouts out.

"Thank you, Dan," Mr. Vann says. He directs four kids to sit on the floor at my feet, and four kids to sit on the floor at Chelsea's feet. Dee Dee's on my team.

"If it's fair!" Dan shouts next.

I'm not about to raise my hand and remind everyone that math *is* fair. Math is exact. It's everything else that's a big, mixed-up mess.

Part of me wants to call out just like Dan. It's fair! Let's agree that it's fair and the answer is four, and move on to the next easily solved problem. The sticky note on my forehead is starting to itch.

But Mr. Vann closes his eyes for a moment. "Elaboration, please, Dan," he says finally.

"Well, let's say Mika is a country and Chelsea is a country, and all those other kids are food or land or whatever. Each country should get four whatevers. But that's not what usually happens. Mika goes over and bashes Chelsea on the head and takes all her stuff."

I smile at Chelsea. She might be a little bit of a Goody Two-shoes, but I want her to know that I would never bash her on the head and take all her stuff.

"Maybe that's why we need math," Dee Dee says, more to the electrical outlet in the wall than to anyone.

"Or," Chelsea chimes in, "let's say Mika is a person and I'm a person."

"A far stretch of the imagination," Mr. Vann says with a wink, "but we'll try."

Chelsea smiles. "What I mean," she continues, "is that people should get equal shares of good things and bad things, like two good things and two bad things. But that's not what *actually* happens. Sometimes people get extra bad things, and that's not really fair, either."

I look over at Chelsea. I have a sneaking suspicion that Dee Dee told her about my mom.

"Ah, yes . . . inequalities," Mr. Vann sighs.

Chelsea smiles at me. But I have to look away because my eyes are suddenly full.

Walking home from the bus stop, I see the coolest stones on the side of the road. It looks like the snowplow scooped them up and left them on top of the snowbank just for me. There are six of them, just sitting there, smooth and shiny. I get this picture in my head of what to do with them. (Guess I'll have to thank Mrs. Poole for that one.)

I pick them up and zipper them into the small pocket of my backpack.

When I get home, Grandma Beau is busy fussing in the kitchen. Mom is resting. I go straight to my room.

First things first, I spread some newspaper on the floor. Mom doesn't care if I do art projects in my room, as long as nothing permanent gets in or on the rug. I grab some tissues out of the box on my desk and make a detour to the bathroom to wet them in the sink. Then I take the stones out of my backpack and clean each one. As they dry, I find my fine-point metallic-gold Sharpie. I give it a few shakes to get it going.

I choose a bluish-gray stone for Mom. It's heavier than it looks and warm as toast after I hold it in my palm for a little bit. I use my calligraphy stencils to write the word *Hope* on it. On Jeannie's, I write *Joy*. Grandma Beau's says *Love*. I make another one for Ella that says *Friend*. I know they're a little corny, but I really like the way they turn out.

And since I have six of them, I decide to make one for Dee Dee and one for Chelsea, too. I draw a tiny fairy on Chelsea's. It's not the head of a pin, but it seems to fit just fine. My *How to Draw People* book doesn't cover fairies, so I just wing it. (Pun intended.)

I'm not sure what to write on Dee Dee's, so I go into my mom's office and open her laptop. I search for "funny science holiday" and up pops a T-shirt that says *HO HO HO,* but each HO looks like a box from the periodic table. HO is the symbol for holmium, which apparently is a rare earth element. (Thank you, internet.)

When I'm sure the marker is dry and won't smudge, I paint over the stones with some clear shellac and sprinkle them with tiny gold glitter. Not too much. Just enough to make them sparkle a little.

Math Journal Entry #11

Choose a variable, any variable. What could the value of your variable be?

Explain your thinking using words, numbers, and/or pictures.

"Are we going camping? Because I see somebody's got their sleeping bags this morning," Grandma Beau says way too cheerfully on Saturday. Ever since the operation, Mom has had trouble sleeping at night. She gets these dark circles under her eyes. Grandma Beau calls them her "sleeping bags."

Mom gives her a weak smile. I try to imagine us going camping again, but it seems like a pretty impossible thing right now.

At least Mom was able to get rid of the surgical drain. I guess her other lymph nodes eventually realized they had to pick up the slack.

She didn't bother to put that appointment on the fridge. I just noticed that before school one day, she still had the drain, and then after school, she didn't. But the scar from the operation bothers her, so she just wears a nightgown all the time, even when it's not the weekend.

Grandma Beau sets a waffle down on the table. I can see that she's added extra-healthy stuff to the batter, blueberries and tiny seeds that look like ants. Mom pushes the plate away an inch. Then Grandma Beau pours her a glass of something thick and vanilla-smelling.

"So what have we got up for today?" Grandma Beau asks.

Since Thanksgiving, Grandma Beau has practically moved in, except for every once in a while when she goes back to her house to pick up her mail. Mom half-heartedly tells her to go home, that we're fine. But Grandma Beau says she was planning on coming for Christmas anyway, so she might as well just stay on.

"I think we could use some groceries." Grandma Beau opens the fridge. It looks totally full to me.

"Mika, you want to come with? It might be good to break out a bit. We could hit a few tag sales while we're at it. Get a head start on all that holiday shopping."

"That's okay," I say. I take my waffle over to the couch and start looking for the remote.

"Okay, then," Grandma Beau calls. "Guess it's just me."

I hear Grandma Beau gathering her keys and mumbling a list to herself. After she leaves, Mom goes back into her room and shuts the door.

I used to think it would be so cool to stay home alone, but now it feels like I'm alone a lot of the time, even when Mom is here.

A few days later, I come home from school to the sound of Jeannie singing and the smell of popcorn. She has the radio tuned to the station that plays holiday songs twenty-four hours a day, starting back in like October.

"Where's my mom?" I ask, dropping my backpack. "Where's Grandma Beau?"

"Out," Jeannie says. "But you and I are officially the decorating committee." She points to a small potted pine tree sitting in the middle of the living room.

Usually Mom and I drive to a farm in Verbank, where

we pick out our Christmas tree and they cut it down for us. There's a barn with hot cocoa and candy canes, and they give rides out to the fields on their tractor.

Jeannie sets a big bowl of popcorn on the table and hands me a large needle threaded with dental floss. "We are making popcorn garlands," she says way too excitedly.

I should probably be doing my homework, but instead, I sit down next to Jeannie and start stringing. Jeannie sings along to the radio. She must know the words to every holiday song ever written, even that super-fast one about the sleigh bells jing-jing-jingling. Like I said, Jeannie is good at filling in the empty spaces.

"This is not as easy as YouTube said it would be," Jeannie says after poking her finger for the twentieth time. "I feel like I'm rehearsing for *Sleeping Beauty*. Mirror, mirror on the wall, who's the fairest of them all?"

"I don't think that's *Sleeping Beauty*," I say.

"I'll get you, my little pretty," Jeannie cackles, pointing her needle at me.

"Also not *Sleeping Beauty*," I say.

With a little practice, Jeannie and I get better at stringing the popcorn. After a while, we *actually* have a string for which the most appropriate unit of measure would be feet, and not just inches.

I hear Mom and Grandma Beau pull up outside. Grandma Beau walks in first, carrying a stack of boxes in her arms.

"I found them online for a song," she says. "But we had

to go pick them up. They're traditional English Christmas crackers. When you pull them open, you get a joke and a paper hat and a silly prize. Isn't that fun?"

Grandma Beau drops the boxes on the table right on top of Jeannie's popcorn string.

"Hey," Jeannie says. "Respect the decorating committee."

Mom walks in next. She seems different, lighter somehow. Then I realize what's changed. Her hair is really, really short.

"You cut your hair!" Jeannie squeals. "Pixie time! It's so cute!"

My mom has had long hair ever since I can remember. That's been a constant. And for a second I feel like Mom with short hair is this big symbol. A reminder that anything can change. Everything's variable.

"We even bought some makeup to cover up those sleeping bags," Grandma Beau says in a fake whisper.

"It looks nice," I say. But on the inside, I'm wondering if my mom's hair is just the first part of her to disappear.

Math Journal Entry #12

Karina is 11. Her mother is 38. (Remember them?)

Devise an algebraic expression that shows the relationship between their ages. Why is your expression "good for a lifetime"?

Explain your thinking using words, numbers, and/or pictures.

Karina's mom will always be _27_ years
older than her.

Let $\boxed{K}$ = 20   Let $\boxed{K}$ = 50

Then M = 47   Then M = 77

The relationship always stays the same.
(The relationship between the numbers, at least.)

$$K = M - 27; \quad K + 27 = M$$

Mr. Vann says that as soon as we take our seats, we can explore the latest math journal consideration. And as soon as we do that, we can start our holiday party.

Chelsea brought in a big platter of fancy cupcakes that I'm sure she made from scratch. Each one has a mini candy cane sticking out from the top. I just brought a bag of chips.

On the way to my desk, I pass by Chelsea's. I reach into my backpack and take out the stone I made for her. I set it down on her desk.

"Happy holidays," I say.

"Awww!" Chelsea says. "Did you draw that? I love it. Thanks, Mika."

Then I head to Dee Dee's desk and give her the HO-HO-HO holmium stone.

She looks down at it carefully. "That's pretty brilliant," she says. She tucks it in the front pocket of her jeans and gives it a pat.

Mr. Vann reaches into his desk drawer and takes out a big bottle of cranberry juice and a package of paper cups. And even though everybody just had lunch, we can't wait for the party to start.

It's dark and gray outside, and school has that puffy feeling of the last day before a vacation, like all the rules are off. Plus, I can't help thinking that the day before vacation might end up being better than the vacation itself.

Usually Mom and I go away for a few days over winter break, like to a museum or to see Jeannie in a show somewhere. But this year, I have a picture in my mind of a blank road stretching out in front of me. It looks all blurry and frozen and empty.

"Someone please give me an expression!" Mr. Vann shouts. "Chelsea's cupcakes are beckoning."

"A stitch in time saves nine!" a kid named Khalil calls out. Then he gives a little grin. "Sorry, but your request wasn't very specific."

"Touché!" Mr. Vann yells. "Somebody please give me an *algebraic* expression at least somewhat tangentially related to our math journal meditation."

He runs to the back of the room and takes one of Chelsea's cupcakes off the party table. He starts peeling back the silver liner.

"The mom is always twenty-seven years older," a girl named Maya explains very quickly. "So you can do *Mom minus twenty-seven equals Karina,* or *Karina plus twenty-seven equals Mom.* Then you can plug in any number. If Mom is thirty, Karina is three. If Karina is thirty, Mom is fifty-seven. If Karina's ninety-nine, her mom is . . ." She takes a minute to do the addition in her head.

"Dead!" Dan shouts from the back of the room. "If Karina is ninety-nine, then her mom is so dead."

Everyone is cracking up and heading to the party table. And even though I'm laughing and eating, too, I can't help thinking about the hardest algebraic expression of all. If Karina's mom is gone, who takes her place?

★ ★ ★

"It looks a little overwhelmed," Jeannie says when she sees our tiny tree fully decorated. I hung the popcorn garlands on it. I also brought up the ornaments from the holiday box in the basement and hung them. Every single one.

Jeannie shrugs. "Overwhelmed might be appropriate."

"We'll do our presents tonight," Mom says. "Just the girls." But this time the girls are me and Mom and Grandma Beau and Jeannie. "Because tomorrow," Mom says excitedly, "there will be presents from Santa." She claps her hands.

I know that Mom knows that I'm getting a little old for the whole Santa thing, but she seems happy. Plus, Santa is really the spirit of Christmas, right?

Grandma Beau grabs a gift bag from the sea of Christmas crackers surrounding our tiny tree. She hands it to me. Inside there are two pairs of socks, which I didn't even know I needed. Socks may sound boring, but one pair *actually* has Monet's *Water Lilies* printed on them, and the other pair has Van Gogh's *Starry Night*.

"Where did you find these?" I ask. "They're so cool."

"Online, of course," Grandma Beau says.

"There's this new thing called the internet," I say to Mom with a silly nod. "Everybody else's parents let them use it."

"Well, good thing I'm not everybody else's parent," she says with her own silly nod back.

Next, Jeannie hands me a small box.

"Sorry," she says in Mom's direction.

I unwrap my gift. It's an iPod Touch. Mom gives Jeannie a look.

"It's not a phone," Jeannie says defensively. "It just plays music. And a few games. And you can text and—"

"Thank you!" I say. I jump up and give her a big hug.

"Okay, my turn," I say. As I'm searching for my three small presents under the tree, the phone rings. Grandma Beau answers it.

"Mika," she calls. "Your father."

I go to the kitchen and trade Grandma Beau her present for the phone.

My dad's not calling from work, but it's still hard to hear him because the dogs are making a racket in the background.

"Merry Christmas, Mika," he says. "Did you get the package from us?"

"Yeah," I say. "But I haven't opened it yet."

"Let me put Katie on," he says. Like he just wanted to confirm that their gift had arrived, but he doesn't have all that much more to say to me.

"Hi, Mika," says Katie. "We miss you. Merry Christmas. I hope we can see you soon. Happy New Year, too."

When I get back to the living room, I see Mom looking down at the stone in her hand. It's so quiet I can hear her breathing.

"Oh, Mika-Mouse," she says.

Each day of winter vacation, Mom seems a little better, more like herself. She cleans the house and helps me set up the real artist easel that Santa brought. She even leaves a message at the town recreation department about an after-school art class for me, starting in January.

We stay up until midnight on New Year's Eve to watch the ball drop, just the two of us. And the next morning, Mom goes into her office, first things first, to catch up on some work.

I can't help thinking that we're in some cheesy story like *A Christmas Carol*. Jeannie was in it last year in Memphis. She played Mrs. Cratchit. And just like in the play, all the good wishes for joy and peace and health and happiness are making Mom better, just like poor little Tiny Tim.

"Mom seems better," I say to Grandma Beau. I'm taking the ornaments off our tiny tree and putting them back into the holiday box. The tree looks almost relieved.

"I guess the break did her some good," Grandma Beau says.

"I'm the one who had a break," I laugh. "Mom's *actually* working right now."

"Oh, that's not what I meant," Grandma Beau says with a wave of her hand. "You know, a break from thinking about her treatment options and whatnot."

I accidentally drop the salt-dough snowman that I made in kindergarten. Luckily, he's a sturdy fellow and falls onto a pile of newspaper.

"I don't get it," I say.

"Well, you know, now that we're through the holidays, she'll start the next phase," Grandma Beau says. Sometimes Grandma Beau says *you know* like I'm supposed to know something that I don't.

"Not going to be easy," she mutters. Then she takes our popcorn garland off the tree and gathers it around her hand. She goes to the kitchen, and I hear her open the cabinet with the garbage can.

I suddenly feel like there's this balloon in my chest that I didn't even know was there. And the balloon just got a huge hole in it and completely deflated. How was I supposed to know there was another variable that I didn't even know about?

"What next phase?" I ask the air. "Why didn't anybody tell me?"

"Vacations are fun, but now it's back to the old grindstone," Grandma Beau says, coming into the living room. "Speaking of which, back to school for you tomorrow."

Unit 7

Fractions

"The average person spends one-third of his or her life asleep," Mr. Vann says as he rummages in the top drawer of his desk. "We are four-fifths of the way through this school week. Approximately one-half of the students in this class identify as girls. One-third of the fifth grade is in Pod Two. The fifth grade makes up one-fourth of the student body at Highbridge Middle School. Approximately one-fourth of you attended Montgomery Hills Elementary. This class is now one-twentieth over."

"Chapter nine." Dee Dee raises her hand. "I'm putting my money on chapter nine, fractions."

"Correct." Mr. Vann smiles at her. "Twenty thousand points for correctly anticipating the question not yet asked."

"Chicken livers," Dan tries.

"Perhaps," Mr. Vann says thoughtfully. "Perhaps."

Mr. Vann closes the desk drawer and leaves the classroom. Then he peeks inside. "Oh, right," he says. "Please move the desks to the sides of the room. I'll be right back."

We all stand up and start moving the furniture. A few minutes later, Mr. Vann returns, carrying one of those huge rolls of brown paper. He sets it down on one side of the classroom and starts unrolling it. Then he gets scissors and tape from his desk and secures a large piece to the floor.

"We are going to create a collaborative fraction mural," Mr. Vann announces. "That is to say, you may draw whatever you'd like, but the items you draw must fit into specific categories. Over the course of the unit, we'll find as many fractions in the scene as we can. For example, one-seventh of the animals might be cats. Two-elevenths of the cars might be blue. Five-fourteenths of the people might not be wearing any shoes."

I get my colored pencils and head over to the corner where Dee Dee and Chelsea are sitting.

"No fair," Dan says as he takes a seat across the mural. "The super-smarty-pants are all in the same group." He uses his pencil to point at me, Chelsea, and Dee Dee.

"I doubt it has anything to do with pants, dear Dan," Mr. Vann says with a smile.

Huh. I never thought of myself as one of the super-smart kids before, especially not in math. But this year, I feel like I kind of am.

Dee Dee starts drawing the solar system above the people I'm working on. Chelsea is drawing different kinds of fairies in the air. One-sixth of them are flower fairies.

"So guess what," Dee Dee says as she draws. "My sister has been begging my parents to go away over February break. Usually I can't stand all her whining, but this time they gave in. We're going to see my cousins in North Carolina." Dee Dee stops talking long enough to draw a huge sun in the sky.

"Hey!" a kid named Peter yells. "I already drew the sun."

Dee Dee draws a smiley face in the middle of her sun. "Now one-half of the suns have smiley faces," she says. She gives Peter a thumbs-up.

"Where in North Carolina?" I ask.

"Don't know," Dee Dee says. "And don't care. As long as it's warmer there than it is here."

We look out the window at the huge icicles hanging down from the roof. "I bet you could spear somebody with one of those things," Dee Dee says.

"Don't forget the sunscreen," Chelsea says with a serious nod. She looks at me as if she's told Dee Dee this on my behalf. It's okay. I know she's just trying to be helpful.

"I'm going to theater camp that week," Chelsea says. "What are you doing, Mika?" It seems we've barely gotten back from one vacation and all anybody can talk about is the next one. I think for a minute.

Mom hasn't sat me down on the couch for another big explanation, but I hear her talking to Grandma Beau and Jeannie and to my dad on the phone.

A few days ago, Mom started the next phase of her treatment. Grandma Beau takes her to the medical center every day while I'm at school. They don't bother writing the appointments on the fridge.

The doctors are giving her some kind of medicine that's supposed to help keep the cancer from coming back. I guess the thing about a bad spot on a peach is that even after you scoop it out, there's a chance that the spot will go bad again.

Grandma Beau says we're lucky because after a couple of weeks, Mom will be able to take the medicine at home, and she won't have to go to the hospital every day. She can give herself a shot "right in the caboose," Grandma Beau jokes. But it's not funny.

It's not the kind of cancer medicine that makes your hair fall out. It just makes your hair a little thin (apparently the reason Mom decided to get hers cut short a few weeks ago). But it does make you feel like you have the flu, and it gives you a whopper of a headache that sends you to bed for most of the day. I won't bother pointing out that the medicine seems to make Mom sicker than the sickness ever did. The side effects are supposed to get better after a while. I just have no idea how long that while is.

Grandma Beau's back at our house 24-7, but she

spends most of the day in front of the computer in Mom's office. Jeannie's off doing a limited run of *Kiss Me, Kate* in Connecticut. Our house is gray and still. It feels like everything is hibernating.

"Earth to Mika," Dee Dee says, giving me a gentle elbow. "What are you doing for February break?"

"Nothing," I say with a shrug. "I'm not doing anything."

But a few days later, a postcard comes from my dad. Mom hands it to me as I walk in the door. "Your dad would like you to come visit over February vacation. I think it will be fun." She says this like she's going to come, too. But I know she's not.

The postcard has GREETINGS FROM ORLANDO on the front. The first O is an orange. The last O is a lemon. The letter L is a palm tree. It all looks so colorful and happy.

"Your dad and Katie would like to spend some time with you." Mom's talking in a fuzzy way.

I turn the postcard over. I read: Hi, Mika. We would love to spend some time with you. Love, Dad and Katie. I can tell that Katie did the writing.

I've never gone to Florida during the school year before. I always go in the summer. Mom says it's less disruptive.

"What about you?" I ask.

Mom sits down at the kitchen table with a sigh.

"I've got Grandma Beau," she says.

"I'm not going anywhere," Grandma Beau calls from Mom's office. "Oh, and Mika, email for you from Ella. She's having a birthday party. Next Saturday at three."

I guess Grandma Beau is checking Mom's email now, too. "Thanks," I say.

It feels a little weird that Ella invited me to her party. It's not like we talk that much anymore. We just pass in the cafeteria and wave a little. Then again, we've always celebrated our birthdays together, so it would probably be even weirder if she didn't invite me.

Mom starts to say something. I assume she's going to ask what I want to do for *my* birthday, which is only ten days after Ella's. In elementary school, our moms would have to coordinate to make sure that we didn't plan our parties for the same weekend.

Usually I put a lot of thought into my birthday party. Last year's theme was Paint in Your PJs. It was basically a sleepover with lots of art projects. Mom found these mini artist palettes with real paints and teeny, tiny brushes to put in the goodie bags.

But I don't think now is the right time to tell Mom I'm getting a little old for that kind of birthday party. I was thinking of just inviting a couple of friends over for pizza and a movie or something. But then I remember that we're not talking about my birthday anyway.

"It will be nice to spend some time with your dad,"

Mom says, like she's the one who's going. She starts rubbing her temples with her fingers.

"Yeah," I answer, and my throat suddenly aches. I can see the algebraic expression the grown-ups are putting together.

Let *Dad* + *Katie* = *Mom*.

Math Journal Entry #13

Use fractions to express a whole idea, in all of its glorious parts.

The cancer comes back in 1 out of 4 people who do the treatments $= \frac{1}{4}$

The cancer comes back in 1 out of 3 people who don't do the treatments $= \frac{1}{3}$

$\frac{1}{4}$ seems small, but not that much smaller than $\frac{1}{3}$. I like to think about it the other way around....

The cancer does not come back in 3 out of 4 people who take the medicine = $\frac{3}{4}$

That is almost a whole paper plate.

As Grandma Beau says,
"That's enough to hang your hat on".

"Who would hang their hat on a plate?" Dan asks. He's peeking over my shoulder on his way to the pencil sharpener.

"You're not supposed to read other people's journals," I say.

"It's a *math journal*," he says with a roll of his eyes. "It's not like it's a real journal."

"Dear thinkers, what is two weeks from Tuesday?" Mr. Vann asks as soon as Dan sits down.

I'm not about to raise my hand and say that it's my birthday. Plus, I'm pretty sure that's not what Mr. Vann is talking about.

Chelsea flips through her day planner. "February second," she answers.

"Not incorrect," Mr. Vann says. "But there happens to be an important city ballot measure under consideration, and although there is still a very long time before you fine young citizens are able to vote, this important decision takes place exactly two weeks from Tuesday."

"What's the vote about?" Dan asks.

"Not sure," Mr. Vann says, "but still . . . *extremely* important. And even more important, it will also be our dear Mika's birthday."

Chelsea's hand shoots into the air. "May I bring in cupcakes?" she asks.

"That is a question," Mr. Vann says, "that does not require asking." Chelsea received four trillion bonus points for her cupcakes from the holiday party.

"And can I *please* make a birthday chart?" Chelsea asks next. "I know it's not a middle school thing, but it would really help me with cupcake planning."

"I would love to say yes," Mr. Vann answers, "but as representing and interpreting data won't be covered until chapter seven, and we are currently stuck at chapter nine . . . But back to fractions. Let's imagine that one-half of eligible voters turn out to vote. And of those, one-fifth vote yes. What fractional part of all eligible voters will have voted yes?"

Dan throws his hands up. "What are they voting about? I think we need some more information before we can tackle the problem."

"Actually," Mr. Vann says, bowing in Chelsea's direction, "you have all the information you need to solve the problem at hand. Let us not get distracted by ruminations that do not serve us or questions that have yet to be asked."

Mr. Vann is right. The actual multiplication is simple. One-half times one-fifth equals one-tenth.

And besides, the whole idea sounds like good advice. I'm not going to think about things that I don't need to think about right now. I'm not going to think about Ella's party and whether it will be weird to be there. I'm not going to think about what it will be like at my dad's over February break. I'm not going to think about how much longer my mom has to keep taking this medicine (one year, to be precise). And I'm not going to think about how much time it will take for everything to go back to normal.

Math Journal Entry #14: Numerate! Denominate!

Devise some fractions, then choose an operation and operate!

ere I am ½ of a
amily.

NY

FL

Mom & me

There I would be
⅓ of a family

(which doesn't even
feel like a family).

Dad, me, Katie, Fritz & Willie

$$\frac{1}{2} - \frac{1}{3} = \frac{3}{6} - \frac{2}{6} = \frac{1}{6}$$

Unless dogs count, too.... If dogs count,
then I'm only ⅕ of a family.

$$\frac{1}{2} - \frac{1}{5} = \frac{5}{10} - \frac{2}{10}$$

That makes me $\frac{3}{10}$ less, which is approximately ⅓
if you estimate (and life is mostly an estimation).

I'm the only person at Ella's birthday party who's not a Onesie. I'm also the only person who brought a present. Apparently, the email said it was "no gifts," but Grandma Beau didn't exactly attend to precision when she communicated the details of the invitation.

Every other kid here probably has her own email address, as well as her own phone to read her own emails on. But I show up at the door with a dorky gift bag and a huge homemade card.

"It's supposed to be no gifts, Mika," Ella whispers to me. She takes the bag and card and drops them on a bench by the door. I hear the *Friend* stone go clunk as the bag lands. (I never got a chance to give it to her at Christmas.) Now I wish I had just left it at home or maybe never made it in the first place.

The Onesies spend most of the party talking about teachers and kids I don't know. Or they don't really talk as much as say things and then start laughing.

"Mr. Hammersmith!" Hysterical laughter.

"David Perez!" Hysterical laughter.

"Peanut butter pretzels!" Hysterical laughter.

After the cake, I tell Ella that I should probably get back home to check on my mom. Then I ask to borrow her phone so I can call Grandma Beau to come pick me up.

Unit 8

Sets and Subsets

Dee Dee sits down across from me in the cafeteria. She, Chelsea, and I eat together pretty much every day now. Then, when we're done, we can just head straight to math.

Dee Dee digs a piece of paper out of her pocket and hands it over. I unfold it. It's a printout of some article from the web.

I read the headline. A scientific study somewhere says that approximately two-thirds of cancer cases can be blamed on plain old dumb bad luck. I skim through the article. It doesn't say that it's okay to start smoking and going to the tanning salon every day. It just says that sometimes there's no clear reason for things.

"Thanks," I say. I fold the paper back up and put it in my pocket. I don't know why, but it makes me feel better.

Chelsea comes over and sets down a plastic container, specially designed for transporting her famous cupcakes. She opens the cover.

"Happy birthday to you!" she sings. "Happy birthday to you!" Dee Dee joins in. "Happy birthday, our dear Mika! Happy birthday to you!"

"I made us each two," Chelsea whispers, taking the fanciest cupcakes out of the container. They're decorated with colorful sugar flowers. "We get one now *and* one in math."

Dee Dee reaches around and pulls a present wrapped in newspaper comics out of her backpack. She hands it to me. "You don't have to wear it," she says with a shrug.

I unwrap it. It's a T-shirt that says: EARTH *Without* ART *is Just* EH.

"No, I *love* it," I say. I pull it on over the shirt I'm wearing. Dee Dee gives me a thumbs-up.

Then we eat our fancy cupcakes and go to math.

Mr. Vann is waiting at his desk. "Prime-number ages demand a certain recognition," he says. Then he reaches into the top drawer and takes out one of his famous tea candles and a pack of matches.

He lights the candle, but he doesn't eat it. I do. (I make sure to blow it out first.) And even then, I don't pop the whole thing in my mouth. I nibble around the wick. (It is white chocolate, by the way.)

Once everyone arrives, Mr. Vann tells us to open our books so we can start a new unit.

"Think of a set as a collection," Mr. Vann begins. He opens his desk drawer and starts pulling things out—a straw hat, the box of matches, a spinner from the game Twister, another pack of paper plates.

"How might we define this set?" he asks.

I look at the collection on his desk. The only words that come to mind are "totally random."

I guess it's no use asking Mr. Vann why he keeps those particular things in his desk drawer, or why he decided to start chapter eight today. Just like it's no use asking the cells in my mom's leg why they decided to get all wacky a few months ago. Or even longer than that. The doctor said the spot on my mom's leg was probably "bad" for a while.

It's also probably no use asking Mom why she didn't go to the doctor sooner. It's like she got the estimation wrong, rounded up when she should have rounded down, or maybe the other way around.

"Am I being punished?"

It's the first thing I hear when I get home from school. Not *Happy birthday!* or *Surprise!* Or even *How was your day, Mika?* Mom keeps asking Grandma Beau the same question, over and over.

I was hoping we would get a pizza and maybe some ice cream at least, but Mom seems to be having one of her "difficult spells," as Grandma Beau calls them.

"Punished for what, honey?" I hear Grandma Beau say. The voices are coming from my mom's room. "Have you taken the new prescription?" she asks. The new prescription isn't for the cancer, or even for the headaches. It's for the panic.

"Is it because I was a lifeguard? Should I *not* have been on the swim team? Would I have been better off rotting my brain in front of some video game?" Mom asks. Her words are coming out so fast, they get all pushed up against each other.

"Have you given any more thought to that support group?" Grandma Beau asks calmly. "Maybe that could help with some of these questions."

"What did I do wrong?" Mom asks. Then she starts to cry.

I hear Grandma Beau go into the bathroom, open the medicine cabinet, then fill a glass of water.

After a few minutes, it gets quiet. Grandma Beau shuts the door to Mom's room and comes into the kitchen.

"It's you and me, kid," she says.

"Just the two of us," I mumble. I walk over to the fridge and open the door.

"No, I mean we gotta go," Grandma Beau says, grabbing her purse. "Dentist time."

"What?" I say.

I shut the fridge door and look at the to-do list. The date at the top is from like three months ago, but scrawled across the rest of the page, it says: *Don't forget—Mika—Dentist Feb. 2* in Grandma Beau's messy writing.

"Who makes a dentist appointment for someone on their birthday?" I ask.

"Sorry," Grandma Beau says. "I didn't know it was on the books. They just called yesterday to confirm, and by then it was too late to cancel."

I tear the sheet off the pad and crumple it up in my hand.

At least the hygienist makes a big deal about it being my birthday. She gives me like five free toothbrushes and a whole handful of mini tubes of the toothpaste with the blue sparkles in it. And luckily, I don't have any cavities.

"Did Mom forget it was my birthday?" I ask Grandma Beau on the way home. I still have that funny taste in my mouth from all the fluoride. It makes me feel like I'm not myself.

"It's not that she forgot," Grandma Beau finally says. "She just didn't put two and two together."

Maybe Mom should try coming to Mr. Vann's class. Maybe her math is rusty because she hasn't been doing a lot of work lately. *Actually,* she hasn't been doing a lot of anything lately. And then she feels bad because she's not working. Then she starts to worry. Then she starts to panic. Then she starts to cry.

I know Grandma Beau has started paying for groceries and shampoo and things like that. And I think my dad's child support is enough to pay for part of the mortgage and things I might need. I guess it could also pay for an after-school art class, but that idea has kind of faded away.

I look out the window and start playing my new game. If I see a yellow car in the next five minutes, things will be back to normal soon. If we make the next two stoplights, everything will be okay.

"How about some birthday soup?" Grandma Beau suggests when we get home. "And I promise we'll do something special this weekend." Grandma Beau reaches into her purse and pulls out a tiny present. She puts it in my hand.

"Thanks," I say.

Then Grandma Beau gets busy chopping vegetables.

I open my gift. It's a tiny ceramic moose baby. Maybe the mom moose and baby moose got separated in the craziness of Grandma Beau's big box of treasures, or maybe they got separated before that. I put the baby next to its mom on my desk. Then I hear the phone ring.

"Mika," Grandma Beau calls from the kitchen. "Can you get it? My hands are full."

I jog back to the kitchen and pick up the phone. It's Jeannie. After she finishes an operatic version of "Happy Birthday," she asks to speak to my mom.

"Mom!" I call. "Jeannie!"

Mom picks up in her room. Through the phone, I can hear that she's crying again, or maybe she never stopped. It sounds staticky and strange, like she's very far away and not just in the next room. Then she asks Jeannie, "What do people do?"

I've heard her ask Grandma Beau the same question. I've heard her ask my dad. I've heard her ask the doctors. "What do people do?"

She asks all the grown-ups. But she doesn't ask me.

Math Journal Entry #15

Create a few sets. Don't forget to "brace" yourself. Then find your subsets.

Remember to use numbers, words, and/or pictures.

(Also remember to bring in a "set" of Valentines for the class next week.)

SET A = Mom, old guy 1, old guy 2, old guy 3, old guy 4

Mom   #1   #2   #3   #4

SET B = Mom

A ⊂ B

SET C = Mom, breast cancer 1, breast cancer 2, breast cancer 3, breast cancer 4

Mom   #1   #2   #3   #4

SET D = Mom

C ⊂ D

The Onesie party

SET E = Me, Onesie 1, Onesie 2, Onesie 3, Onesie 4

me   #1   #2   #3   #4

SET F = me

E ⊂ F

Mom feels like her own subset.

(Sometimes I do, too.)

"Who's up for sharing?" Mr. Vann asks.

He keeps looking at the clock like he can't wait for class to be over. It's the Friday before February vacation, and Mr. Vann seems more excited than any of the kids to get the day over with.

Nobody raises a hand. It's quiet.

Dan is absent again. He loves to "shave," as Mrs. Poole calls it. He manages to shave off a day or two on either side of a vacation. I'm not sure where he went this time.

My mom, of course, made my flight to Orlando for Saturday morning. No shaving for me.

"Who would care to share?" Mr. Vann tries again. "Because sharing is caring." Everybody groans.

"Have we forgotten this a mere twenty-four hours after such protestations of love and affection?"

Yesterday, Mr. Vann let us have a Valentine's Day party. We got to make mailboxes out of paper lunch bags, and Chelsea brought in cupcakes with little candy hearts on top.

Then we passed out our Valentines. But they had to have some kind of math message, like *Without You, I'm < 0* or *You are as sweet as* π. My favorite was the one from Dee Dee. She had the symbol for pi saying: *I'm just not rational when I'm with you.*

"Fine," says Mr. Vann. "We shall create subsets out of the set of all of you dear thinkers. Then you shall share your sets and subsets with each other within your respective subsets. And due to the fact that in exactly four hours and twenty-nine minutes, I will be on a nonstop airplane heading due south, you may feel free to choose your own subsets." Mr. Vann pulls a straw beach hat out of his desk drawer and plops it on top of his head.

Dee Dee and Chelsea hurry over to my desk.

"I did something about the matter and antimatter from black holes," Dee Dee explains. She has a million mathematical formulas all over the page in her journal. It's probably worth about a zillion bonus points, but I don't understand any of it.

Mr. Vann paces the room, peeking out from under his straw hat and eavesdropping on our conversations. He looks down at the page from Dee Dee's journal. I assume he's about to give her the zillion bonus points, but instead, he reminds her that variety is the spice of life.

"Remember, Dee Dee," he says as he walks away, "there is more to the universe than just . . . the universe."

Chelsea seems to have anticipated Mr. Vann's advice and decided against making sets and subsets about her notebooks. She did something about cooking and the ingredients you need for different recipes. "I'm coming to your house for dinner," I say as a joke.

Meals at my house have pretty much disappeared. Mom used to make such a big deal about us sitting down at the table to eat. Even if it was "just the girls." But now I usually bring my plate to the couch and eat in front of the TV.

"Super!" Chelsea says with a smile. "You can both come."

"I'm in," Dee Dee says with a nod. "Okay, Mika, your turn to share because remember—sharing is caring."

I look down at the page in my math journal.

"My mom," I start, "went to this support group for people who have the kind of cancer she has, but all the other people were old men. So she's her own subset."

"Makes sense," Dee Dee says. "Cancer's just more common in old people."

"So then she went to a women's support group, thinking that it couldn't be all old men. But all of those women had breast cancer."

Chelsea blushes a little when I say *breast,* but Dee Dee doesn't care. I always thought Dee Dee would become an astrophysicist or something, but I can see that she would also make a really good doctor. She doesn't get all embarrassed about that kind of stuff, and she's good at talking to people.

I think my dad is a good doctor when it comes to the science-and-being-smart part, but he's not the best at the talking-and-listening-to-people part.

I see Dee Dee peeking at the picture of the Onesies in my next example. "So we'll make our own set," she says matter-of-factly.

"What do you mean?" Chelsea asks.

"Our own *set,*" Dee Dee says, like saying it again explains what she means. "But we'll need a name."

"Like the Onesies?" I ask. "My friend Ella, she's in this group called the Onesies."

"I've seen them," Chelsea says. She fidgets with the top button of her sweater.

"They talk a lot about clothes and TV and who likes who," I say.

"Who likes *whom*," Chelsea says. She smiles apologetically.

"Thanks," I say. "Who likes *whom*."

"Some of those girls were in my class last year," Dee Dee says. "I used to think if I wore a dress once in a while, they'd like me."

This is weird because Dee Dee doesn't seem like the kind of person who worries at all about who likes *whom*.

"We could be the Twosies," Chelsea suggests weakly.

"Nah," says Dee Dee. "Let's give it some time. Then we can come up with a really awesome name."

"How about the Please Get Outta Heres?" Mr. Vann calls over to us.

We look up. Everybody else is gone. I didn't even hear the bell that sounds like a horn, and Chelsea and I are probably going to be late for gym. But I don't care.

I quickly draw a big empty circle on the next page of my math journal. It's a space for our new set. I'll fill it in later.

Only Grandma Beau brings me to the airport on Saturday. Mom's "just not up to it."

When I land in Orlando, a short three hours and ten minutes later, Katie's there to pick me up. She waves to me with a rolled-up poster covered in plastic.

"It's a poster," she says, taking my bag from me and handing me the roll. "Well, obviously it's a poster. I thought you might want to put it in the guest room. I mean, your room. But no worries if you don't. Sorry your dad couldn't be here. He got called in to the hospital. Are you hungry? You must be hungry."

All I'd had was orange juice and a tiny bag of pretzels on the plane.

"Actually," I tell her, "I'm really hungry."

Katie steers me toward a restaurant right there in the airport. Mom would never let us eat in the airport. "Not a good value," she would say. "Captive audience means inflated prices."

Katie looks around for the hostess stand.

"Are you sure?" I ask her. "I mean, I can wait until we get to your house."

"You're human," Katie says with a smile. "You need to eat. Besides, we're not going straight home."

The hostess seats us, and Katie orders us each an iced tea.

"Don't take this the wrong way," she says, looking over the menu. "But the kids' meal looks really good. I say go for it while you still can."

After we order, Katie reaches into her very large handbag and pulls out a plastic shopping bag. She sets it in the middle of the table. Then she pushes it toward me. I take the bag and look inside. There's a bathing suit and a tie-dyed beach dress.

"Couldn't help myself," Katie says with a smile. "Plus, we have a lot of swimming to do this week, you and me. I hope they fit. If not, we can exchange." She reaches for the tag on the swimsuit and looks at it closely.

"It was snowing in New York," I say.

"Which reminds me," Katie says, pulling her phone out of her bag. "Call your mom, please. Let her know you're here safe."

I dial, but it rings and rings and then it goes to voice-mail.

"Hi," I say. "I'm here." I hang up.

Katie picks up the poster from where it's leaning against my duffel bag. She hands it to me. I pull off the plastic wrap and unroll it.

"I know you're a big Monet fan, and it's not a Monet," Katie says with a fake frown. "It's Matisse. But I saw it and I liked it."

The image is a figure, reaching up. Everything about it is uneven, but strong at the same time, solid. The background is bright blue, and there are yellow stars all around. At least, I think they look like stars. The figure is solid black with a red circle where its heart would be.

"I like it, too," I say.

After lunch, Katie and I go to the Orlando Science Center.

"It's so on our way home," Katie explains, "we kind of *have* to go."

After looking at some dinosaur bones, Katie says we

should "hit the gift shop." I find a package of astronaut ice cream for Dee Dee and a tiny box of gemstones for Chelsea.

Then we get tickets to see a 3D movie about the ocean. The theater is super air-conditioned and dark, and the seats are really comfortable. You can lean way back in them. I watch the fish swim toward me. Without even meaning to, I reach out to try to touch them.

Behind the plastic glasses, it's easy to forget about everything. It's easy to feel fine.

When I get to my dad and Katie's house, my dad's on the phone. He gives a wave and holds up a finger, which is code for "Be right there." Then he points to the phone and mouths, "Your mom."

Katie helps me bring my things to the guest room. Their dogs, Willie and Fritz, follow us and jump up on the bed. They nearly crush two really pretty gift bags that are sitting there with about a million ribbons tied to the handles.

"Belated happy birthday," Katie says. Then she tugs on the dogs' collars. "Get down, you two monsters." But instead of getting off the bed, the dogs just lie down on top of it.

"I suggest keeping your door closed," Katie says, scratching Willie behind the ears. "Or you will have friends."

"It's okay," I say. I sit down next to Fritz. He's warm and panting and stretches over to lick my face.

"Time to open your presents," Katie says, sitting down next to me. She seems very excited. "Oh, I hope you like it."

"Shouldn't we wait for my dad?" I ask. I can hear him in the hallway still talking to my mom. But the "Mika's here" part of the conversation has ended. Now I hear things like "remember Felicia from med school?" and "new cutting-edge trial" and "advanced genetic targeting."

"Well, you can open the one from me," Katie says. She pulls a gift bag out from under a dog and puts it on my lap.

Inside is a set of professional-looking colored pencils and a big blank book. The cover says: *Creativity Takes Courage.*

"I was thinking maybe you'd like to make a scrapbook while you're here," she says. "But it's just an idea. No worries if you're not into it."

"Thanks," I say.

My dad appears in the doorway with the phone still in his hand.

"Your mom will call back," he says.

"Okay, now open the one from your dad," Katie says. She leans over and gives him a fake punch to the arm. "We have a little wager going."

I pull the tissue paper out of the other gift bag. It doesn't seem like there's anything inside. I reach down deep and find a piece of paper. It's a receipt for a family membership to the Orlando Museum of Art. It's good for two adults living in the same household and their children.

"So who wins?" Katie asks. "Seeing art or doing art?"

"We're so glad you're here, Mika," Dad says.

Last summer, that would have gotten a major eye roll from me. I would have told Mom about it when I got home, and it would have gotten a major eye roll back from her. But now I'm kind of glad he says it. Katie reaches over and gives my hand a squeeze. Then the phone rings again.

"Barnes here," Dad says, sounding official. He walks into the hall.

"Looks like it might be just us," Katie says. "Let's take these monsters to the dog park before dinner."

Katie lets me sit in the front seat of the car. Mom won't let me sit in the front seat until I'm twelve, but Katie says there's no reason I should have to squish between two stinky dogs in the back.

At the park, I throw Willie and Fritz a ball and a Frisbee. Then I sit down on a bench to draw with my new pencils. It seems like the light here is different. And everything's green, even in the middle of February. I don't know if I would want to live here all the time, but it's nice to have a break from the cold.

"So tell me about middle school," Katie says, sitting down next to me. "Who's your favorite teacher? Who's your least favorite teacher? What's happening? I want to know everything."

I tell Katie about Mr. Vann and how it's weird that math is my favorite class this year. I tell her that we don't do any drawing in art because "drawing" is not part of the fifth-grade curriculum. I make those fake quotation marks in the air. Katie rolls her eyes and sighs, like she can't believe what she's hearing.

"My mom's looking into finding an art class after school," I say. "But she's still working on it."

I wait for Katie to tell me that my mom has a lot on her mind and that I need to be patient and understanding, but instead, she just asks more questions.

"And tell me about your friends. How's . . . What's her name? Ellie?"

"Ella," I say. "We have this thing called pods in middle school, and she's in a different pod, so . . ."

"Okay, so not Ella," Katie says. She makes a swiping motion with her hand like she's moving Ella to the side and making space for something new.

I tell her about Dee Dee and her funny science shirts, and Chelsea and her fancy cupcakes.

"We're thinking of making like a club," I tell her.

"An art club?" Katie asks.

"No," I say. "I guess it's more like a math club."

"Totally cool," says Katie. "But you'll need a good name."

★ ★ ★

The next day, my dad has to go into work, so just Katie and I go to the museum.

The Orlando Museum of Art doesn't have Impressionists, no Monets or Renoirs, not even anything by Matisse, but they have lots of other cool artists.

There's one painting I really like called *Below Albany*. It was obviously *not* painted in February. The caption says it's from the Hudson River School, so not French, but a little closer to home. I love the sky over the river, soft and wispy and exactly right.

In one of the galleries, there's a workshop going on. It's supposed to be for little kids, but Katie talks the teacher into letting us have some supplies. We each get a clump of clay and a bunch of feathers.

Katie makes a bird. I make a collection of tiny fairies.

Math Journal Entry #16

Set it up with two different sets.

What's the union? What's the intersection? Show what you know!

Please use numbers, words, and/or pictures.

Union

Home ∪ Florida = (Mom, me, Dad, Katie, Willie, Fritz)

Intersection

Home ∩ Florida = (me)

Just me

Grandma Beau and Mom pick me up at the airport on Saturday. For a second, I think it's so nice that they both came to get me. But when we get to the car, I notice that Grandma Beau is the one doing the driving.

"So?" Grandma Beau asks in her trying-not-to-be-nosy way.

"It was fun," I say. "Katie gave me some really nice colored pencils. I drew too many pictures of Willie and Fritz. Dad had to work a lot."

Grandma Beau gives a little snicker. "Surprise, surprise," she mutters under her breath.

"It's warm there," I say. "Like there's no winter."

"How was the flight?" Grandma Beau asks. "Did your ears bother you?"

"No," I say. "I had gum."

"Did they pick you up at the gate?" she asks next. "I hope they picked you up at the gate."

"Katie did," I say. "Oh, and I got some new shoes. They're slip-ons, but they're really soft, and they have a little heel. It's only like an inch. Katie thought I was old enough for a little heel, but she said that if you thought the heel was too . . ."

I stop talking because it feels like Grandma Beau is using all of her energy to get us out of the maze of the parking garage. Mom has her head resting against the passenger-side window with her eyes closed. It feels like my voice is evaporating somewhere between the back seat and the front seat. And even though I just got home, I still feel very far away.

That's one thing about measurement that we never covered in chapter four. How it's possible to feel so far away when you're only sitting a few feet back. We also didn't learn how one really big problem makes all of your other problems seem pretty small.

The size of that heel seemed so important when Katie and I were talking about it. It took us a long time to pick out those shoes. And we made sure to put the receipt in a safe place in case we needed to return them. (I taped it into my scrapbook.)

When Grandma Beau pulls out of the parking garage, the sky is thick and gray. It's already almost dark, even though it's barely five o'clock, and I can't help thinking that in Florida it would still be afternoon and bright. Willie and Fritz would be camped out on some couch or bed where they're not supposed to be. My dad would probably be at work, but Katie would be fixing us dinner. I would be sitting at the table working on my math journal or my scrapbook.

"Do you have homework?" Mom asks distractedly, like it's a regular day, and I didn't just get off a plane after being away for a whole week.

"Just math," I say. "I already did it."

Unit 9

Advanced Computation and Order of Operations

"There are approximately fifteen chapters in our faithful textbook," Mr. Vann announces as he pops in the door at 1:01. "As we unfortunately did not have time to start a new unit right before the vacation, we will have to start one right after."

"But we didn't share our last math journal entries," Chelsea says.

"Let's not and say we did," Mr. Vann says, "because today is sure to be one of our busiest days of the year. Today is the day we complete four chapters in one day."

Mr. Vann starts rummaging around in his desk drawer. He doesn't find what he's looking for, so he walks over to the storage cabinet in the back of the room.

He opens the cabinet door and pulls out a pocket calculator that looks like it was made sometime in the 1980s.

He walks across the room and drops the calculator on Dan's desk, but Dan's not there. He's shaving again.

The bulky plastic thing lands with a clattering sound. It doesn't seem to be any worse for wear. It's probably indestructible.

Mr. Vann goes back to the cabinet and manages to locate a few more ancient calculators. "Please open your books to chapter ten, chapter eleven, chapter twelve, or chapter thirteen. Take your pick. Makes no difference to me."

I open my book to chapter ten, *Advanced Computation: Addition,* then chapter eleven: *Advanced Computation: Subtraction.* Chapter twelve is *Advanced Computation: Multiplication,* and chapter thirteen: *Advanced Computation: Division.*

"Can I just use the app on my laptop?" Dee Dee asks, pulling her computer out of her backpack.

"Can I use my cell . . . Oops!" a kid named Eliza says before she remembers that she's not supposed to have her phone at school in the first place.

"But of course," Mr. Vann says. "I've only got ten of these beauties." He holds the calculator like he's trying to sell it in a commercial. A bunch of kids sheepishly take phones out of their bags and pockets.

"Please select some problems from the book and start pressing buttons," says Mr. Vann. "But get it out of your systems now, because after today, it's back to the past, where the only technology available will be paper, pencil, and your mind." He taps his finger against his forehead.

"And today, you may choose your own groups because even though variety is the spice of life, sometimes you might feel like something not so spicy."

Chelsea takes out her phone and brings it over to my desk. I can't believe she's actually breaking the "phones stay home" rule. But I bet her mom makes her carry it for emergencies. Dee Dee brings her laptop over to my desk, too.

"I just thought of a name for us," Dee Dee says first thing. "All break, I couldn't think of anything. It's like trying to find a name for a band, and there are no good band names left. But it just came to me. Don't think of it as corny—think of it as *retro.*" She waits a minute and takes a deep breath. "The Calculators."

"I love it," Chelsea says, smiling. "It sounds like the name of a movie. Like when they make a movie about us."

"It's awesome," I say. "The Calculators. It fits."

"Dee Dee, Chelsea, and Mika," Mr. Vann calls over to us. "A little less human communication, please, and a little more mindless data entry."

Mr. Vann continues roaming around the room. "When I was a student, we didn't have smartphones or tablets or laptops." I can't help imagining a young Mr. Vann walking to school, clutching his math journal to his chest.

"In fact," he continues, "the power of the computer that got man to the moon can now be found in the tiny phone that Dylan is using to text his friends over in Pod One. OMG. LOL."

When Mr. Vann stops talking, it's quiet except for the hum of kids whispering and the clicks of keys tapping. The sound is soft and busy and full.

I sense someone behind me, looking over my shoulder. I assume it's Mr. Vann peeking at my work, making sure I'm attending to precision. But when I turn around, Mr. Vann is all the way at the back of the room. He's busy cleaning out the storage cabinet that the ancient calculators came out of.

"Good day, Highbridge students." It's Principal Mir. She must be wearing her quiet shoes today because I didn't hear her clicking when she came in. She takes out her tiny notebook and writes something down.

I look around the classroom. The way I see it, 50 percent of the class is breaking the "phones stay home" rule, 40 percent is breaking the "laptops in lockers" rule, and the other 10 percent is just chatting. I know we haven't gotten to percentages yet, but however you add it up, it doesn't look good. I'm a little worried for Mr. Vann.

"Greetings, Principal Mir," Mr. Vann calls from the back of the room. He takes a break from cleaning out the storage cabinet. He doesn't look very concerned. "Lovely day, isn't it?"

I look out the window. It looks like it's snowing sideways.

Principal Mir just nods, returns her tiny pencil to its place behind her ear, and leaves the classroom.

Math Journal Entry #17

"Calculators are the greatest invention since sliced bread."

—OR—

"Calculators make middle school students lazy."

Make your case. (Then put your calculator in it.)

I don't think calculators make us lazy, or any lazier than we already are. Unless all you use them for is problems you could just as easily solve yourself. But I don't think they're really meant for those kinds of problems.

Calculators are more like handy support when you're working through a very l o n g ⟷ and complicated problem.

And yes, they are the ☆ GREATEST ☆ thing since sliced bread!

The Calculators

"Calculators are extremely effective," Mr. Vann announces, "for finding the correct answer."

Dan is finally back from February vacation. He makes a big deal of writing this down, like Mr. Vann has just shared the biggest secret of the universe.

"However," Mr. Vann continues. He's walking around the room, collecting the plastic calculators and returning them to the newly organized storage cabinet. He jokingly swipes Chelsea's phone from the top of her desk.

At the beginning of the school year, she would have gotten really upset. But now she just holds out her hand. "Neither a borrower nor a lender be," she reminds him.

Mr. Vann does a little sleight of hand to give Chelsea her phone back. "However," he repeats, "calculators are somewhat less effective for tackling innovative problems and embarking on reflective discussions of relevant math topics."

"That's what math journals are for," Dee Dee adds.

"I challenge you, dear thinkers," Mr. Vann announces, "to produce a word in the English language that rhymes with . . . PEMDAS." The first syllable rhymes with *stem*. The second syllable rhymes with *brass*.

"Are you sure you want us to answer that?" Dan asks with a smirk. "I mean, the first thing that comes to mind is obviously phlegm-a—."

"Point taken," Mr. Vann interrupts. "Moving on. PEMDAS is not a word. It is an acronym. It is a road map to guide us through the choppy waters of a complicated problem."

I won't point out that you don't use a road map to guide a boat, but I get Mr. Vann's meaning.

"What's an acronym?" a girl named Helena asks.

"Dee Dee?" Mr. Vann nods. "Care to assist."

"An acronym is a word created by the first letters of its component definition," Dee Dee explains. "For example, NASA stands for National Aeronautics and Space Administration. Or laser—Light Amplification by Stimulated Emission of Radiation."

"Precisely," Mr. Vann says. "PEMDAS is an acronym to help us remember the order of operations. Because *when* we do something, dear thinkers, is just as important as *what* we do, perhaps more so. PEMDAS stands for . . . Well, I think I'll let you figure that out. Please find a group and work together to create a reasonable definition for PEMDAS. And no opening your textbooks!"

Dee Dee, Chelsea, and I meet up in our regular corner.

"The first official Calculators meeting is Saturday," Chelsea announces. "I asked my mom. Five o'clock. My house. I'm cooking." She smiles, and Dee Dee and I nod, and that's that.

"Could it possibly be *Pie Every Monday, Donuts All Sundays*?" Mr. Vann asks as he strolls around the room. "Or *People Everywhere Make Decisions About Sandwiches*? Or maybe it's *Persnickety Elephants Manufacture—*"

Mr. Vann is interrupted by a loud ding-ding-ding. You might think that was the bell, if you forgot that the bell sounds like a horn, but it's the PA system.

The voice of Ms. Alice from the main office fills the room. "Mr. Vann?" she says. "Sorry for the interruption."

I'm trying to remember if today is an early-dismissal day and Mr. Vann has forgotten to dismiss us early. That happened last time there was early dismissal. Ms. Alice had to call to find out why none of the kids from Mr. Vann's Grade Five Pod Two Math Block C were on the buses.

"Copy," Mr. Vann says toward the little speaker by the door.

"Do you have Mika Barnes in class?" She says the first syllable so it sounds like *my*.

"No," Mr. Vann says. "But I do have a *Mika* Barnes." He pronounces my name correctly.

"In any case, could you send her down to the office, please?" Ms. Alice asks.

I feel a shiver go up my spine. I've heard people use that expression before, but I've never actually felt it.

"My mom?" I say, more to myself than anyone else.

"Want me to go with you?" Dee Dee asks.

"It's probably nothing," I say, but I don't know if I believe that. Ms. Alice loves her PA system, but she doesn't call you out of class for nothing. I pick up my stuff and leave the room.

I can hear my own footsteps going down the hall. They're echoed by a click, click, click from behind. I turn around and see Principal Mir disappear into Mr. Vann's room.

It feels like it takes me forever to reach the main office. When I finally get there, Ms. Alice is standing at a filing cabinet while talking on the phone. She has an incredible ability to hold the phone in the crook of her neck while she does a million other things.

Ms. Alice smiles at me in a school-office-friendly way and points to a door labeled "Counselor."

I am totally confused. Am I supposed to walk in? Why am I here? Should I just go back to math? Then the door opens.

"Hello, Mika," says a man. "I'm Mr. B." He smooths down his tie, which is decorated with snowpeople playing baseball.

Mr. B motions for me to come into his office and sit down. He has a miniature sofa that looks like it came straight out of the same catalogue as the ones in the waiting rooms at the hospital.

"Hello, Mika," Mr. B says again. "I just wanted to introduce myself and say hello."

"Uh, hi," I say.

"How are you today?" he asks.

"Uh, fine," I say.

"Your mom and I thought it might be helpful for you to have someone to talk to." He pauses. "You know, about what's going on at home, a little support from the High-bridge Middle School community."

I don't know what to say. I didn't know my mom had called Mr. B. I guess it's another one of those things she just forgot to tell me.

"So how are you, Mika?" he asks.

I don't know what to say to that, either. The answer seems way too complicated to explain to a man who thinks that snowpeople can play baseball.

Should I tell him that I'm excited about going to Chelsea's on Saturday? Should I tell him that I'm happy in math? That I'm sad at home? That I really liked being in Florida? Should I tell him that I'm sick of my mom be-ing sick? That I'm great and I'm terrible and I'm just fine and I'm mad and I'm really, really scared?

When I don't say anything, Mr. B says, "Is this a good time to check in? Maybe once a week?"

"Um . . . ," I start.

This is all so middle school messed-up. Grown-ups are always saying how important it is for kids our age to feel like we're part of a group, to feel safe and cozy in our home pods. And then when you finally do, they call you down to the main office.

"No," I say, louder than I mean to. "I mean, it's my math block, and math is kind of challenging for me," I lie.

"Understood," Mr. B says with a smile. "Let me take a look at the schedule, and we'll find another time." He looks down at the large day planner open on his desk.

There are so many names penciled in, erased, rewritten. It makes me feel a little better to see all of those names, to know I'm not the only one with problems.

"You know, Mika," Mr. B says, erasing my name from its little slot. "Sometimes keeping a journal can be helpful during difficult times. A journal can be a place to record and process your thoughts and feelings."

"I have a journal," I say a little too quickly. I don't mention that it's a math journal. But he's right. It does help.

And then I say something I never would have imagined saying before this school year. As politely as I can, I ask, "Could I please go back to math?"

The whole bus ride home I thought about pushing open the door and asking Mom when she was planning on telling me that she had talked to Mr. B.

I was going to say, "Did it just slip your mind . . . like my birthday?" Or "Didn't you think I might like to know I was going to get called out of class *before* I got called out of class? Because *when* you do something is just as important as *what* you do, perhaps more. I know you thought you were helping, but that got canceled out by not telling me first."

I was going to describe how it felt walking down to the main office. How scared I was. Not scared that I was in trouble or anything, but scared that something bad had happened. I mean, that something *new* and bad had happened.

But when I walk in the front door, Mom is at the kitchen table talking to Jeannie loudly. She sounds upset. "I don't understand why they couldn't have just done the last procedure first, and then we could have started this all at least a month earlier."

Mom stops when she sees me.

"Welcome, Mika," Jeannie says, bowing dramatically. I can tell she's trying to "steal focus" from my mom's minor meltdown.

"Hi," I say.

Jeannie's not working right now so she comes over a lot, I think to give Grandma Beau a break. At least when Jeannie's here, Mom comes out of her room and sits at the kitchen table. Mom drinks tea while Jeannie swipes at her phone and looks for funny things to talk about.

Jeannie's phone buzzes. "You must be nuts if you think I am going to Minnesota in April," she says to the screen. "I love *Brigadoon* as much as the next gal, but I am *way* too old for snow on Easter."

I know it's just an excuse. It's not like the weather here is any better. It's still gray and cold. It feels like waiting.

Jeannie looks back down at her phone. "You have got to see this video, Mika. A kitten gets totally freaked by a salamander. Oh, and we're going out for dinner this weekend." She starts swiping again.

I drop my backpack and go to the fridge. I open the

door and stare inside. Jeannie obviously stopped at the deli and stocked us up with yummy things.

"There's a new restaurant downtown," Jeannie goes on. "Or maybe it's an old restaurant under new management. Anyway, it was on one of those food TV shows. Oh, I hope it's not the show where they find a really bad restaurant and try to turn it around. That *never* works."

"Mika," Mom says, like she's on autopilot. "Fridge."

Really? I want to shout. Really? It's so important that I close the fridge door to save the four cents on electricity, but it's not important for you to tell me that the school counselor was going to call me out of math today? But I don't say it. I just shut the door hard.

Mom turns and gives me a look.

"Sorry," I mutter.

"Great," Jeannie says. "Then it's settled. Saturday night. They're supposed to have excellent eggplant. And we're going to have fun. Or at least we'll fake it till we make it."

"But . . . ," I start. Then I stop.

The idea suddenly pops into my mind that if I don't go out with "the girls" on Saturday, something bad will happen. I'm not sure what.

Maybe I should have checked with Mom before telling Chelsea I could come over. That's what I always would have done in the past. When Chelsea asked me, I would have said, "I just need to ask my mom first." Maybe *I'm* the one doing things all out of order.

"It's okay," I say out loud. "I'll call Chelsea and tell her I can't go."

"Can't go where?" Jeannie asks.

"I kind of had plans to go to my friend Chelsea's house on Saturday. But it's not important."

"Hang on," Mom says, putting her mug down. She takes a deep breath. I'm surprised to hear her voice so clearly. Lately, she's like this flat, silent outline. "We can drop you at Chelsea's, and then the boring old ladies will go and have their eggplant," she says in her Mom-trying-to-be-funny way.

"Hey," Jeannie says with a fake huff. "Speak for yourself."

Math Journal Entry #18

Karina and her mother are back. Karina's mother wants to compute the complicated problem below. However, she is unsure how to proceed. Please offer her some direction.

Explain your process using words, numbers, and/or pictures.

$4 + (5 \times 2) - 3^2$

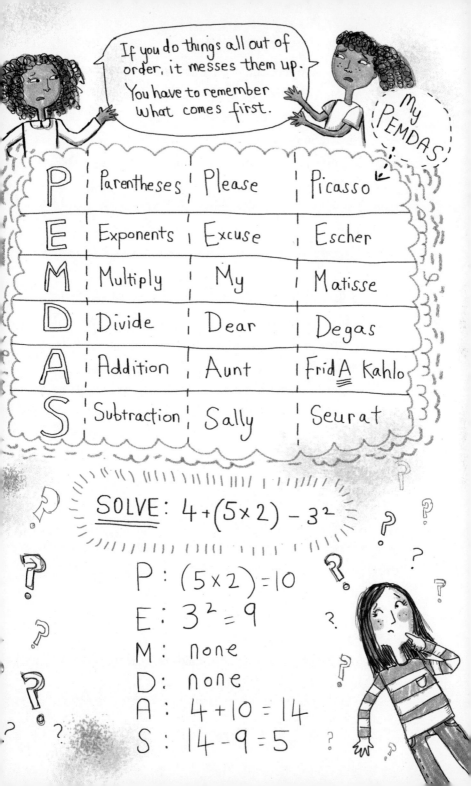

Chelsea's mom opens the door and invites me in.

"I'm so happy to meet you, Mika," she says. "I'm Erica. I've heard so much about you."

Chelsea comes running to the door and gives me a big hug. She leads me into the living room, where Dee Dee is sitting on the sofa, riffling through her backpack. Dee Dee waves without looking up. "Where are they?" she mutters.

"This is the living room," Chelsea says, like she's a tour guide.

One wall is lined with shelves to display all of Chelsea's family's "treasures"—seashells and pretty rocks and tons of snow globes. Grandma Beau would have a field day offering to buy it all so she could resell it online.

"My mom collects snow globes," Chelsea explains with a bit of an eye roll. "Whenever we go someplace, she brings back a snow globe. Even if it's a place that doesn't have snow." She picks up a snow globe with the Hollywood sign in the background to illustrate her point. She turns it upside down and right side up again. We watch the tiny white confetti fall onto palm trees.

Chelsea's mom has been to a lot of places. My favorite snow globe is the smallest one. It's the size of a golf ball, and inside there's a teeny, tiny Eiffel Tower. The base is painted with the skyline of Paris.

"You went to Paris?" I ask.

"No," Chelsea says. "My mom did. But I *so* want to go."

"Me too," I say.

"So we'll go," she says with a smile.

"Okay," says Dee Dee. "But before you go, I have these for you." She pulls three cards out of her backpack. They're about the size of a credit card, and they're laminated. She hands them out.

I look down at mine. Across the top, it says *The Calculators* in a funky font, and in the corner there's a photo that looks just like one of Mr. Vann's ancient calculators. At the bottom there's a blank line, and underneath the line it says, *Official Member.*

"You need to sign," Dee Dee says very seriously. She fishes around in her backpack for a pen.

"Wait," Chelsea says. "This calls for a Sharpie, fine tip."

"Exactly," I say.

Chelsea runs to her room and comes back with a marker.

I carefully sign my card and shake it a few times to make sure the ink has dried. I tuck it in my pocket and give it a pat for safekeeping.

I suddenly realize that I didn't bring anything to our first official meeting. A "hostess gift," as Grandma Beau would say. But even Grandma Beau forgot to remind me about something I needed that I didn't know I needed.

"I'm sorry," I say. "I didn't bring anything."

"The best present is your presence," Chelsea says with extra corny sauce.

"No biggie," Dee Dee says with a shrug. "Just means the next meeting is at your house."

Unit 10

Surfaces and Solids

"Today, dear thinkers, we enter the art of math."

Mr. Vann reaches into the storage cabinet, which is somehow already a complete mess again. He pulls out three boxes of charcoal art pencils and a large stack of thick drawing paper.

"One to a customer!" everyone shouts.

Mr. Vann passes the pencils and paper out himself. "Serious thinkers need serious tools," he reminds us.

When he gets back to the front of the room, Mr. Vann reaches into his desk drawer and takes out a pair of 3D movie glasses. They're just like the ones I still have from my trip to Florida, the kind with one red lens and one blue lens.

"What allows us to see in three dimensions?" Mr. Vann asks mysteriously.

We all know this is not the kind of question he really expects us to answer, although Dee Dee could probably explain it if we needed her to. "And what, dear thinkers," he continues, "is the difference between a surface and a solid?"

Mr. Vann writes the following words on the board: circle, square, triangle, rectangle. He waits until he's sure we have all read the list. Then he erases it with his right hand as he writes with his left: sphere, cube, pyramid, rectangular prism.

He reaches back into his desk and pulls out a box of toothpicks and a bag of mini marshmallows. More serious tools, I guess.

The Calculators meet in our corner. Dee Dee starts building pyramids out of marshmallows and toothpicks. Chelsea stares at one of her notebooks very intensely, trying to draw a rectangular prism with very little height.

I never thought about art and math having that much in common before, but if Principal Mir came into the classroom right now, she'd probably think she'd wandered into the art studio by mistake, except for the fact that people are *actually* drawing.

I'm not sure which solid to start with. I know the formula for a cube. You just follow the steps, and it turns out like it's supposed to. That's easy.

Instead, I decide to try a sphere. It takes time to get the three dimensions of it. It's all shading and shadows. It's mostly trial and error.

★ ★ ★

At home, it's like walking into the same still life every day. Mom is sitting at the table. Grandma Beau is standing at the sink, and Jeannie is talking, talking, although I don't really hear what she's saying. I know I said that Jeannie is good at filling in the empty spaces, but everything feels so tight lately, it's like there's not a lot of space left to fill.

After I get home from school, I usually grab a snack and then go to my room to do my homework or draw. But today the phone rings while I'm still in the kitchen.

"Who could that be?" Grandma Beau asks. "Everybody's already here." I guess that's supposed to be a joke.

I look at the caller ID and see Katie's name. Cool. Maybe she's calling to ask how my new shoes worked out, or maybe she's calling because the dogs did something really cute today, or maybe she thought of a name for our "math club." I probably should have let her know that we came up with a really good one, but I didn't even think of it.

"Hi," I answer. "I should have called you."

"Hi, Miks." It's not Katie. It's my dad.

"Oh, hi," I said. "I thought you were Katie."

"Nope," he says. "Just me. My phone's out of juice. How's things? Listen, can I talk to your mom for two seconds?"

"It's Dad," I say. "For you." I point the phone in my mom's direction.

"I'll get it in the other room," she says blankly. She gets up from the table and walks away.

I guess my dad is another one who could use a little bit of a math review because they talk for way longer than two seconds.

Math Journal Entry #19

Choose a three-dimensional object, any three-dimensional object.

First, represent your object using two-dimensional figures. Next, describe each of the figures you have used. What else can you discover from this solid?

Explain your thinking using numbers, words, and/or pictures.

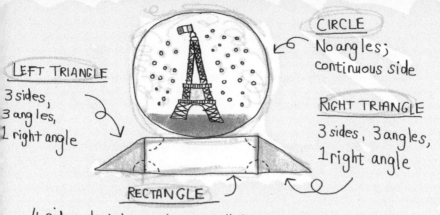

CIRCLE
No angles;
continuous side

LEFT TRIANGLE

3 sides,
3 angles,
1 right angle

RIGHT TRIANGLE

3 sides, 3 angles,
1 right angle

RECTANGLE

4 sides, 4 right angles, parallel sides of equal lengths

If I found the surface area, it would tell me how much wrapping paper Chelsea would need to wrap the snow globe and give it to me.

Just kidding! (not about the surface area but about giving it to me)

If I found the volume of the sphere, it would tell me how much water it would take to refill the snow globe with water from the Seine when Chelsea and I go to Paris.

When Dee Dee, Chelsea, and I get to math at 12:57, Mr. Vann is already there. He's moved the desks and chairs to the sides of the room again and is making a huge grid on the floor with blue painter's tape.

The right angles aren't perfect, and some of the squares are slightly bigger than others, but it's still pretty good. Then he starts rummaging through his desk drawer. He takes out a roll of red painter's tape.

"Thank goodness you're finally here," he says as if we're late and not ten minutes early.

Mr. Vann pulls out a long piece of the red tape and gives me the edge. He gives the rest of the roll to Dee Dee and orders us to separate, separate, separate. Chelsea directs us to keep the line as straight as possible.

Dee Dee and I keep walking backward and away from each other until she's standing against the desks on one side of the room and I'm standing against the desks on the other side. In between, we are holding one very long piece of red tape. You could safely use meters to measure it.

"We need an x-axis, please," Mr. Vann says.

"How many quadrants?" Dee Dee and I ask at the same time.

"Jinx," Dee Dee whispers.

"Great minds . . . ," Mr. Vann says. "Four quadrants, please."

Dee Dee and I carefully lay the long strip of red tape in the middle of the blue grid, side to side.

By now, other kids have started to arrive. They have to sit on top of the desks to stay out of the way of the major construction project going on.

Mr. Vann then has us put down the y-axis, and we now have a huge piece of graph paper . . . on the floor.

Mr. Vann goes back to his desk drawer and finds a plastic bag of big, colorful numbers. They look like something you'd see on a kindergarten bulletin board. It turns out they're stickers. He enlists a bunch of kids to stick the numbers on the grid in the right order, and we're good to go.

"First," Mr. Vann announces, "we warm up."

He starts stretching side to side and touching his toes. "We will start with the technical challenge: Last one to the correct quadrant is a rotten egg. Quadrant One! Go!"

"Wait! What?" Dan shouts.

Everyone scrambles down from the desks and runs to the area of Quadrant One. There's a lot of confusion and tripping and noise, and tons more exercise than we've been getting in gym. Even though it's slightly less freezing outside, the fields are still too muddy and squishy. We usually just sit in the gym to watch videos about healthy living.

"Quadrant Four!" Mr. Vann shouts next, and the chaos erupts again. "If your birthday is in January, February, or March—Quadrant One! April, May, and June— Quadrant Two! You get the idea."

"If only we had a birthday chart!" Chelsea shouts before darting to her quadrant.

We've barely managed to complete the birthday challenge when I see Principal Mir poke her head in the doorway. I can't imagine it looks very good to have the floor covered with tape and sweaty fifth graders.

"Hello, Mr. Vann," Principal Mir calls.

"Hello, Principal Mir!" Mr. Vann shouts back. "Don't worry. This is just the warm-up. Now, shoes with laces—Quadrant Two! Shoes with Velcro—Quadrant One! No shoes at all—Quadrant Four." Dee Dee kicks off her sneakers and hops to Quadrant Four.

"And . . . please sit!" Mr. Vann shouts.

Everyone's huffing and puffing and smiling. When I look over toward the door, Principal Mir is gone.

"That concludes our warm-up," Mr. Vann continues. "Now we are going to talk about ordered pairs. No, Dan," he says, even though Dan hasn't asked anything. "Ordered pairs are not pairs of things you ordered. Ordered pairs are clues, insights, directions. They help us to know exactly where we are."

Mr. Vann reaches into his desk drawer and pulls out his straw hat. Today, it's filled with small pieces of paper. He starts passing the hat around.

"One to a customer," he whispers.

I pick a slip of paper out of the hat and pass it on. My paper has the ordered pair (-2, 5) written on it.

"Once you have your directions, please find your place

on the plane," Mr. Vann says. Dee Dee, Chelsea, and I all end up in the same quadrant. Now, what are the chances of that? But as probability won't be covered until chapter five . . .

"The Calculators rule!" Dee Dee shouts really loudly.

Everybody looks at her like she's totally crazy. Except for Chelsea, who raises a pretend glass and shouts, "Hear! Hear!"

But I think what she's *actually* saying is: "Here! Here!"

And I am happy to be here at (-2, 5). Right now, I can't imagine anyplace else I'd rather be.

Math Journal Entry #20: Ordered Pair Dot-to-Dot

Create a four-quadrant coordinate plane on a piece of graph paper. (Tuck this into your math journal.) Then draw an image, any image, on your coordinate plane. Make sure the outline passes through various points that can be described by ordered pairs.

Record the list of the ordered pairs on a separate page in your math journal.

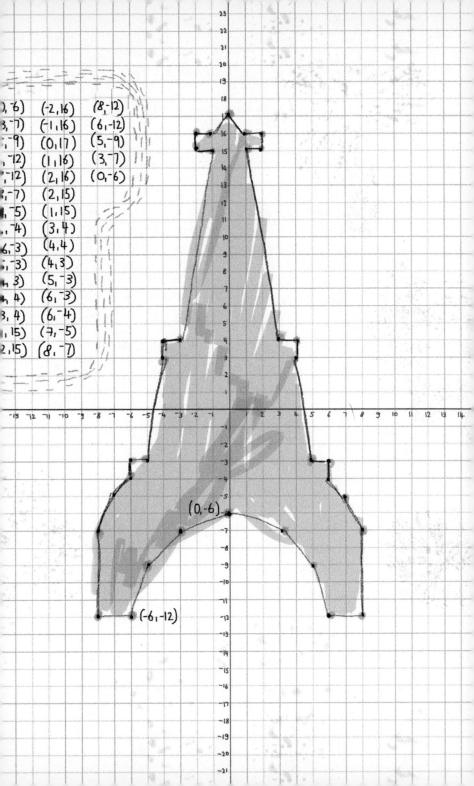

), ¯6)   (-2,16)   (8,¯12)
3,¯7)   (-1,16)   (6,¯12)
,¯9)   (0,17)   (5,¯9)
,¯12)   (1,16)   (3,¯7)
,¯12)   (2,16)   (0,¯6)
,¯7)   (2,15)
,¯5)   (1,15)
,¯4)   (3,4)
6,¯3)   (4,4)
,¯3)   (4,3)
4,3)   (5,¯3)
4,4)   (6,¯3)
3,4)   (6,¯4)
,15)   (7,¯5)
2,15)   (8,¯7)

(0,-6)

(-6,-12)

The phone wakes me up. It's only six-thirty. At first, I think it must be my dad calling before he goes to work. I hear Grandma Beau say hello. She doesn't say anything else. Then she hangs up.

Grandma Beau quietly walks over to my door and peeks in.

"I'm awake," I say.

"Oh, Mika," she says, like I surprised her by being in my own room. "No school today."

"What?" I sit up in bed.

"Snow day," says Grandma Beau. "Well, not snow precisely, but there's a leak or something, so no school."

I look out my window. The snow in the yard is almost melted. On the edge of the flower bed, I can see one teeny, tiny purple crocus poking up. Maybe winter really is almost over. Maybe things do change. Maybe things can get better.

About an hour later, the phone rings again. This time it's Dee Dee.

"My parents have to work and my sister still has school," she says before I even have a chance to say hello. "So I'm coming over to your house."

That reminds me that the next meeting of the Calculators is supposed to be at my house anyway, so why not today?

This time, I remember my order of operations and ask Mom if it's okay first. She surprises me by saying she thinks the idea is super-dee-duper. I have to roll my eyes at that one.

I call Dee Dee back. "Bring your math journal," I tell her. Then I call Chelsea. They both arrive by nine o'clock.

"I love your room," Chelsea says.

"Where's your graph paper?" Dee Dee asks.

I take a few sheets out of my desk and pass them out.

"One to a customer," I say.

Then we sit on the floor and trade math journals. I do Dee Dee's ordered pair dot-to-dot, Dee Dee does Chelsea's, and Chelsea does mine.

After a while, Mom pokes her head in. "You do realize it's a little odd to be doing your math homework *voluntarily,*" she says in her Mom-trying-to-be-cool way. She sets a big bowl of grapes on the floor in the middle of us.

"Oh, we're not doing homework," Chelsea says. "We already did it. But we haven't had a chance to share yet."

"And sharing is caring," Dee Dee says, doing her best Mr. Vann imitation. She turns the page in Chelsea's math journal. The list of ordered pairs goes on and on. "And I'm going to need more graph paper," Dee Dee says with a sigh.

"Sorry," Chelsea says with a smile. "Guess I got a little carried away."

"That was all the graph paper," I say.

"I have some in my office," Mom says. "I'll go grab it."

It feels good to have friends over and have Mom bring

us grapes and try to act cool. It feels normal. I guess Mom is finally getting used to the medicine.

"Thank you, Mika's mom!" Dee Dee calls after her.

Dee Dee's ordered pair dot-to-dot turns out to be a volcano. Underneath it, she's written: All you need is lava.

Chelsea's is a very cute teddy bear.

When Chelsea finishes mine, she cries, "The Eiffel Tower! *Oh là là. Très jolie!*"

We color in the pictures with my colored pencils from Katie. Then we hang them all on the fridge with about a million magnets.

Dee Dee has to stay for dinner because her parents won't be home until after six. We call Chelsea's mom to ask if she can stay, too.

So dinner is "just the girls," which today are me, Mom, Grandma Beau, Dee Dee, and Chelsea.

"After dinner I'm heading home for the night," Grandma Beau says. "I desperately need to check on my treasures."

"And some of us have to work in the morning," Mom says with a sigh. She says it in a way that makes it sound like she's not looking forward to it, even though I know she is. Kind of like if I were to say, "Oh, no, I have math tomorrow."

"And some of you have school in the morning," Mom continues. "At least I think you do." She looks over at the phone and screws up her face, as if to say who knows what's going to happen.

"Luckily, all homework has been completed," I say, and give a silly salute.

Mom gives her own silly salute back. Then she points at my graph paper dot-to-dot, now firmly stuck to the refrigerator with a big bubble-letter *RM* at the top, thanks to Dee Dee.

"Hey, the Eiffel Tower," she says.

"Chelsea's mom's been there," I say.

"And Mika and I are going," Chelsea says. She throws her arm around my shoulder. "We just have to grow up and get jobs and earn enough money first."

"Hey, what about me?" Dee Dee asks like she's really offended, even though I know she's not.

"You're coming, too," I say. And I swing my arm around Dee Dee's shoulders. "All three of us are going."

It's not until I'm in bed that night that I start worrying about what I said. I didn't mean to say that I would go to Paris with my friends and not with Mom.

Unit 11

Real-World Problems

"We have a problem," Chelsea says. She plops her tray down next to mine on the cafeteria table. "I saw a piece of paper."

Usually Dee Dee would say something funny, like "Oh, no! A piece of paper! Whatever will we do?" But we can tell by the speed of the words coming out of Chelsea's mouth that this is no time for jokes.

"My mom had a school board meeting last night. I saw the agenda from the meeting on the table, and one of the action items was a status report from the search committee for the new fifth-grade math teacher."

I don't understand what Chelsea is talking about. There are three Pods, and each Pod has its own fifth-grade math teacher.

"New fifth-grade math teacher," Chelsea repeats. "For Pod Two."

"What?" Dee Dee practically shouts.

"I think Mr. Vann is getting fired," Chelsea says quietly. "And I think it's my fault."

"How is it your fault?" I ask.

"At the beginning of the school year," Chelsea says, "I told my mom about the shouting out and the lighting candles and the not doing the chapters in the correct order. It seemed important back then."

"It's not your fault," I say. "This was probably set in motion long before you were on the scene."

"Thanks," Chelsea says.

"They can't fire a teacher just because one student complains," Dee Dee adds. "Especially if it's an informal complaint to one's own parent who happens to be on the school board." But Dee Dee's confidence seems to decrease the more she talks. "They can't just fire him," she says in a way that begs us to tell her she's right.

"You're right," I tell her. "They can't just fire him." Although we really don't have enough information to know if that's true.

We start packing up our lunch stuff even though we've barely eaten, and we head to math.

"What is today?" Mr. Vann asks. He starts pacing in front of the board. "Come on. Shout it out. There is not nearly enough shouting out in this classroom."

The class starts shouting out answers. Just then, I see

Principal Mir walk by the door, making her rounds. Great, I think, just when the whole class is yelling at the top of their lungs.

"Thursday!" someone yells really loud.

"Probably." Mr. Vann nods. "But as probability is chapter five and we are only at chapter six, we will hold off on the whole 'It's probably Thursday' for the time being."

"I'm pretty sure it *is* Thursday," Dan says.

"Yes." Mr. Vann smiles. "As we said, the chances are high, but let's stick to chapter six for now."

"I think it's a B-day," someone tries next.

"Not incorrect," Mr. Vann says, but he's still pacing and obviously looking for a different answer.

"Is it an early-dismissal day?" Dee Dee asks.

Mr. Vann turns to the clock with a look of concern. "Sure hope not," he says.

"Is it somebody's birthday?" Chelsea asks with her own look of concern. "I would have made cupcakes if I'd known. I sincerely think we should make a birthday chart."

"I cannot disagree," Mr. Vann says. "But seeing as how representing and interpreting data is clearly chapter seven, and we are *still* at chapter six . . ." He lets his voice trail off.

There are more guesses. "Almost Easter?"

"Yes and no," Mr. Vann says.

"A week till April Fools' Day?"

Mr. Vann doesn't say anything. He just opens his desk

drawer, takes out a sticky note, writes something on it, and puts it back in the drawer.

I turn to chapter six. Then I raise my hand, not high enough to pop my shoulder out, but high enough for Mr. Vann to see. He nods at me.

I look down and read directly from the textbook: *"It is necessary to know the problem at hand in order to discern the specific information needed to solve it. For what purpose is this information required?"*

"I thought you'd never ask," Mr. Vann says. "I am planning my next trip to the opera. If I purchase my ticket at least fourteen days in advance, I can save a bundle." He rubs his hands together. "I, of course, cannot go on a school night. Way past my bedtime. April vacation begins, I believe, Monday, April twenty-second. But that, as we all know, is only one week after tax day, and I will have had my hands full. So let's make my date for the theater Tuesday, April twenty-third. What is today? I beseech you, dear thinkers."

"You still have plenty of time to get the discount," I say.

"Whew!" Mr. Vann pretends to wipe sweat off his forehead with the back of his hand. "It's *La Traviata*, after all. Now, I realize our steadfast textbook calls them 'real-world problems,' but I much prefer the term 'story problems.' More dramatic. So please find your groups to brainstorm some characters, settings, and plot points for your own stories."

Before we've even sat down, Mr. Vann calls, "Chelsea, could I please speak with you for a moment?" Chelsea gets up and goes over to his desk. He takes out a sheet of paper and points at it. It looks like he's asking her questions and she's answering them.

"I wonder what that's about," I say.

"Beats me," says Dee Dee.

I tell myself that Mr. Vann has called Chelsea over to talk about the birthday chart and not about the school board meeting.

Math Journal Entry #21: Story Problems

Write a short story. (Emphasis on the word *short*—this is math, not language arts, after all.) Infuse your story with numbers. Then create one question that CAN be answered using the information in your story, and one question that CANNOT be answered. But DO NOT answer them! (We will do that together.)

Professor X spends 10% of class time on parties  and cupcakes and magic tricks

Some people (including Principal Y and certain members of the School Board) think that this is too much time spent on silly stuff

However, Professor X's class scores 20% higher on The Big Test than any other class.

When Professor X only spends 5% of class time on parties and cupcakes and magic tricks, his class scores 10% higher on the Big Test.

As soon as I finish my math journal entry, I wish I'd chosen something else to write about. I'm worried that Mr. Vann is going to read it over my shoulder and wonder why I'm writing about him. It's pretty obvious he's Professor X, even though I technically used a variable.

I wonder if Mr. Vann knows they're looking for a new fifth-grade math teacher for Pod Two. Would it be better if he did know? Maybe I should cover up the page in my math journal with my elbows. Or maybe not. Maybe if he knows now, he can make a plan, and things will be better later.

And that's another thing chapter four failed to teach us about time. How sometimes bad things now can turn into good things later, the same way good things now can turn into bad things later.

But my elbow-cover-up strategy doesn't matter because Mr. Vann doesn't have us share our short stories or even trade math journals with a partner to answer each other's questions.

Today actually *is* an early-dismissal day, so math is a mere seventeen minutes long. And in what is maybe the strangest math class of the entire year, Mr. Vann just assigns us a list of problems from the textbook to work on quietly. Then he sits at his desk and fills out something that looks like paperwork.

When I get home from school, Mom is sitting at the kitchen table. She has her own stack of paperwork in front of her. I don't see Grandma Beau around.

For a small second, it feels like how things used to be. In elementary school, after Mom picked me up at the bus stop, we would go home and have a snack. Then she would bring her work to the table, and I would work on my homework while she worked on her work-work.

"Where's Grandma Beau?" I ask.

"She went home to check on some things," Mom says. "She'll be back."

Mom gathers up her papers and pats the chair next to her for me to come sit.

"Listen, Mika," she starts. "I want to talk about the treatments. They're the reason I've been so fatigued and crabby and altogether . . ."

"Absent?" I try. I know it's a school word, but it seems to fit.

"Yeah," she says with a sigh. "Absent." She messes up my hair, but just once. "So the doctors have been giving me a little break from them. My numbers weren't too good."

So far in math this year, we've learned about large numbers and real numbers and rational numbers and imaginary numbers and positive numbers and negative numbers. But we haven't learned about good numbers and bad numbers.

"I could stop them altogether," she says. "Then maybe things could get a little bit back to normal."

"You can do that?" I ask.

She nods. "They recommend a whole year. But they also said the side effects would abate . . . I mean go down."

"I know what *abate* means," I say. I don't say it meanly. I'm not trying to be fresh. I just want Mom to know that she doesn't have to change the words for me. I'm old enough to understand.

"But if you stop them early," I say, "the chances of the cancer coming back go up."

"Uh, yeah," Mom says again. She seems surprised that I know so much about it, that she's not my only source of information.

I wait a bit before asking my next question. "But if you stop the treatments, are they *sure* it will come back?"

"No," she says, "but the chances are slightly higher."

"Define slightly," I say.

Mom rolls her eyes.

"I'm serious."

She pulls a paper from the bottom of her stack. *"This study indicates that the therapy lowers the risk of a recurrence from approximately thirty-seven percent to approximately twenty-six percent,"* she reads out loud.

I knew these numbers before. I estimated them as fractions in my math journal back in Unit 7, and here they're expressed as percentages, but they haven't changed.

"Eleven percent," I say. "About one-tenth. That's like a slice of a large pizza."

"I guess that's one way to look at it," Mom says with a chuckle.

"What do the doctors say?" I ask her.

"They recommend the full year, but they also say it's my decision." Mom sighs. "I don't think they really know. I don't think . . ."

"I don't think we have enough information to answer this question."

"Yeah," Mom says.

"Yeah," I repeat. "Some questions are like that."

Math Journal Entry #22

Imagine you do not have all the necessary information to solve a real-world problem. What could you do?

Explain some strategies for dealing with this mathematical conundrum.

Dear Mr. Vann,

I know the answers you are looking for.
I did read Chapter Six, and I have been
paying attention in class.
I know what you want me to say:

1. Estimate.

2. Make an educated guess.

3. Refer to a similar problem.

4. Do some research.

But sometimes there are questions that
you don't have enough information to answer.
There are problems that you really don't
have enough information to solve.

It's not that the information is missing
and you're going to find it somewhere
else.

It's that the information actually
doesn't exist.

I have done some research, and here are the strategies I've found for this type of conundrum, mathematical or otherwise.

When Dee Dee and I get to math a few days later, the door is locked. The little strip of glass is dark, and not just because the lights are off inside the classroom. There's a piece of cardboard stuck in the window, like when we have testing or a lockdown drill. I'm wondering if this is some kind of April Fools' joke.

Dee Dee and I look at each other.

"What's going on?" Dee Dee asks.

"No idea," I say.

I know we're ten minutes early, but we've never gotten to math to find the door locked before. I look around for Chelsea, but she's not here. She wasn't at lunch, either. Dee and I assumed she was absent.

But now that I think about it, Chelsea got the Montgomery Hills Elementary School Perfect Attendance Award five years in a row, and unless she was physically unable to walk or unconscious somewhere, she would be at school.

"Maybe they already did it," I say quietly.

"Did what?" Dee Dee asks.

"Fired Mr. Vann," I say.

"That's crazy," Dee Dee says. She has her face up against the door, trying to peer around the paper in the window.

But it doesn't seem that crazy to me. It seems perfectly logical. They fired Mr. Vann and hired a new teacher who doesn't leave the classroom open for kids who would rather be in math than the cafeteria; another teacher who can't write and erase the board at the same time; another teacher who will do the chapters in the textbook in the right order. And when Chelsea found out, she felt like it was all her fault, and she felt so bad that it made her sick, and she had to stay home today.

I see someone coming around the corner at the end of the hallway. It's Principal Mir. She walks toward us with her click, click, click.

"Can I help you, ladies?" she asks when she gets close enough to speak to us in an "inside voice." The question sounds funny, like she's working at a coffee shop and she's ready to take our order.

"We're waiting for Mr. Vann," Dee Dee answers.

"Did you have an appointment?" Principal Mir asks next. She takes her pencil from behind her ear and her little notebook from her jacket pocket.

"Uh, not really," Dee Dee says.

I want to explain that this is what we do every day. I force myself to get the words out. "Um, we come to math early," I say quietly, "but usually the door is open." I hope I don't sound like I'm trying to make trouble.

"That's fine," Principal Mir says. She jots something down, and then tucks her notebook back into her pocket. "Just please be aware. We do have a rule about loitering in the hallway." Then she walks away.

"I really don't like that word," Dee Dee says under her breath.

"What word?" I ask.

"*Loitering*," Dee Dee repeats. "It sounds like *toilet*

backward. Besides, would she rather we be *loitering* somewhere else? I don't understand how we're getting in trouble for coming to class too *early*."

"Because everything is all messed up," I say.

"Do you really think he's gone?" Dee Dee asks.

I think about her question for a minute. Would they *actually* fire Mr. Vann before the end of the school year? Were things so terrible that he had to be removed immediately? Was he that dangerous? Maybe they were worried about his ways spreading, so they scooped him out just like a bad spot on a peach.

"I'm glad Chelsea's not here," Dee Dee says. She's still trying to get a look into the classroom. "She would feel like it was her fault."

Suddenly, the classroom door opens. Luckily, it opens inward or Dee Dee would have gotten bonked right in the nose. As it is, she stumbles forward into the classroom. I step back.

It's not Mr. Vann at the door, and it's not a new teacher, either. It's Chelsea.

"Bonjour," she says, completely seriously. *"Bienvenue à Chez Vann*. Table for two?"

"Huh?" Dee Dee says. Her jaw has literally dropped.

"So sorry to keep you waiting, but you do realize we *actually* don't open for lunch until one-oh-seven." She points up at the clock.

Chelsea opens the door wide enough to make it click and stay. Then she turns on the lights.

The classroom has been transformed. The desks are pushed together into tables for four. There is a red-and-white-checked tablecloth on each one. There are paper plates and plastic silverware, and along the counter at the back of the room, there are two huge casserole dishes and a big platter of Chelsea's famous cupcakes.

"Why, yes," Dee Dee says in a fake French accent. She doesn't miss a beat. "We *actually* do have a reservation for two, under the name *Les Calculators.*" She emphasizes the last syllable and draws it out.

"Right this way." Chelsea giggles. She hands us each a photocopied menu and leads us to a table.

There are three items on the menu—baked ziti, garlic bread, and cupcakes. There's a note at the bottom stating that there is a 6 percent restaurant sales tax and a mandatory 18 percent gratuity.

"And please enjoy this special offer," Chelsea says, handing us a slip of paper.

It's a welcome coupon for 10 percent off our first visit to Chez Vann.

"We are a self-service buffet, but please do write down what you have ordered, and as far as the cupcakes go—one to a customer."

Other kids start to arrive. Chelsea leaves our table and goes to seat another group. She gives them menus, coupons, and instructions.

Then, at exactly seven minutes after one, Mr. Vann appears in the doorway.

"Table for one," he says seriously.

Before he sits down, he goes over to his desk and takes out a small portable radio. He turns it on and tunes it to the classical music station.

No one would believe that we had all just come from lunch because everyone's stuffing their faces. Chelsea made the food, so of course it's delicious. The music on the radio is a piano piece, and everyone is sitting and eating and chatting, just like at a real restaurant. Even Dan plays along. He flags Chelsea over and asks her to give his compliments to the chef.

"The only downside to this lovely meal," Mr. Vann announces while dabbing the corners of his mouth with a napkin, "is that tabulating your check is also self-service. If your party calculates its check accurately, your meal is on the house. Discount is taken pretax, and it is polite to tip on the full check and not the discounted amount. And beware of those pesky decimals. But do feel free to round to the nearest hundredth. Real-world problems often call for a little estimation."

Dee Dee turns her menu over, and we start calculating. She circles all of our answers and signals Chelsea that we're ready.

"Sorry I didn't tell you," Chelsea says as she passes by. She puts her hand on her heart. "Mr. Vann swore me to secrecy."

Chelsea picks up our paper and brings it to Mr. Vann,

who now has a toy cash register on his desk. He looks over our calculations, then gives us a wink and a thumbs-up.

"Thank goodness," Dee Dee says. "I don't have any money with me."

"So that's why Mr. Vann needed to talk to Chelsea the other day," I say.

"He's not fired," Dee Dee says with a smile. "Well, not yet."

When I get home from school, I start telling Mom and Grandma Beau about Chez Vann and the baked ziti and the cupcakes and Chelsea, the hostess. I tell them how if you didn't figure out your bill correctly, then you really had to pay. Dan, unfortunately, did not attend to precision, and ended up owing ten dollars and forty-one cents.

But as I babble on about the tablecloths and the radio and the toy cash register, I realize no one is saying anything. No one is laughing. No one is asking questions. The quiet is back, louder than anything.

Mom is sitting at the table and staring out the window with that blank look on her face. She has her hands clasped around a mug. She looks like a painting if you printed it out in black-and-white. Like when the color cartridge is empty and you have to print using only the black ink. It's just different tones of gray.

"That sounds great, sweetie," Grandma Beau says distractedly.

It takes me about seven seconds of elapsed time to figure out that Mom has restarted her treatments. I don't know how she made the decision, and I don't know when she made it. All I know is that she didn't tell me first.

Grandma Beau hands me a big envelope off the kitchen counter. The return address is my dad and Katie's. I rip it open as loudly as I can. Mom doesn't even seem to notice.

Inside the envelope, there's a page of Care Bear stickers, a pencil with a huge pink feather where the eraser should be, and a tiny notepad made out of cool origami paper. On the first page, it says, "Couldn't resist the Care Bears. Would you *care* to visit us again? Love, Dad and Katie." The handwriting is Katie's.

"When were you planning on telling me?" I ask. I cross my arms in front of my chest. I feel my foot tapping against the floor. Like I'm the parent and my mom is in big, big trouble.

"Tell you what?" Grandma Beau asks.

I keep looking at Mom, waiting for her to answer.

She turns her head from the window, like she's slowly coming into focus, like she's just now realizing that I'm home, that I'm here.

"It just came today, Mika," she says, vaguely pointing at the envelope. "Your father didn't know you had time off from school, and when I told him you had . . . what's it called?"

"April vacation," I snipe. "It's always called April vacation. You *know* it's called April vacation. It's been on the calendar since September, and that's not what I mean."

"Well, you know we've been chatting with your father," Grandma Beau chimes in, "about some medical decisions."

I know Grandma Beau is just trying to help, but I don't want her to explain my mom to me right now. And I don't want her to tell me what I already know. I want Mom to explain herself.

Plus, I hate it when Grandma Beau starts calling my parents "your mother" and "your father." Like I'm the one responsible for this whole mixed-up mess.

"And then when we telephoned your father to tell him that your mother had decided to resume . . ."

"You told *him*?" I say. For some reason, this makes me the maddest. "You told *him*?" I say again. "You decide what to do and you don't tell *me*?"

"Mika," Mom starts. But I don't let her finish.

I run to my room and slam the door. I throw the stupid envelope on the floor and plop down on my bed. I make my hands into fists and stick my fists in my eyes. I dig my elbows into my knees. I don't even feel like crying. I just feel like . . .

When I start seeing weird shapes, I move my hands. It takes a moment for my eyes to focus. I stare down at the floor.

The rug in my room is full of little things that should not be in a rug—two pieces of dried-up rice, one of those teeny-tiny safety pins, a square of old Scotch tape, something that looks like cat hair even though we, of course, don't have a cat. There are still some specks of tiny gold glitter from my Christmas stones, and even a shriveled-up grape that must be left over from the Calculators' meeting about a million light-years ago.

I slide down to the floor and peel up the piece of tape. I try to use it to pick up the rice and the mystery hair, but the tape is too old. It's lost all of its stickiness.

Then I get an idea. I take the sheet of Care Bears stickers out of the envelope. I pull them off as fast as I can. I don't care if they rip. One by one, I slam them against my dirty rug. They pick up most of the disgusting stuff. I use every last sticker, and then ball up the whole linty mess and throw it against the wall. It just comes back at me. I throw it again, this time against the door.

The confusing thing is, I like the idea of going to Florida again. I like the idea of swimming and going to the museum with my family membership. I like the idea of talking to Katie about normal things and small problems, like shoes and friends and school. I like the idea of talking to Katie, period.

Plus, Katie's carpet doesn't have enough crumbs to feed a pet parakeet. My dad and Katie's house is clean. It's messy because people live there and they have big dogs and they do things besides stare out the window. But it's clean because someone takes care of it. Someone takes care of things.

Katie's house is clean and it smells like lemons and anyone who's sick is called a patient and gets left at the hospital when my dad comes home from work.

Our house is neat, but that's because nothing moves, nothing changes.

I hear a knock at my door. Mom opens it a crack before I even say she can.

"Mika-Mouse?" she says softly into the open space.

She opens the door a little more.

"It's just . . . ," she starts, but her voice cracks. "I don't want to look back and think there was something else I could have done."

I don't want to tell her that I understand. I understand how bad things now can turn into good things later. I don't want to tell her anything. I just want this all to be over.

I am tired of playing the game in my head that says if I get mad, something bad will happen. Something bad already happened, and I *am* mad. I'm mad at everything, and mostly I'm mad at Mom. I'm mad at her for getting sick.

I slide over and push the door closed with my foot.

"Mika," Mom says from the other side.

"Leave me alone," I mumble. "I have homework."

Unit 12

Representing and Interpreting Data

I barely talk to my mom over the next few days, except to tell her that, yes, I have done my homework, and, no, I don't need her to help me pack for Florida. It's like her quiet is contagious and now I've caught it.

And just when it feels like nothing is ever going to change, I wake up this morning and it's like we skipped spring and went right to summer. It's warm as toast and all the trees seem to have gotten their buds overnight.

At lunch, everyone heads straight outside. Even Dee Dee, Chelsea, and I barely make it to math on time.

Most of the class is late. If I had to express it in a fraction, I would estimate that about two-thirds of the kids straggle in after the bell, all panting and sweaty.

As Dan rushes in, Mr. Vann starts drawing a huge chart on the board. He writes Monday in the box in the top left corner. Then he turns around and waits. When it's finally quiet, he looks up at the clock on the wall and writes 1:12 p.m. in the next box.

"I challenge you, dear thinkers," he announces, "to produce a word in the English language that rhymes with *data*." He pronounces the first syllable so that it rhymes with *day*.

Everyone starts muttering, trying to come up with something. No one bothers asking why we're trying to think up rhyming words in math.

"Beta," Dee Dee blurts out.

"Not incorrect," Mr. Vann answers. "But I believe I did specify a word in the English language, and as beta comes to us originally as the second letter of the Greek alphabet, I am going to rule: BUZZ!" Mr. Vann makes a loud sound like the buzzer that tells you you're wrong on a game show.

"Can I please go to the nurse?" Dan says as he raises his hand. "I think I *ate a* bad clam at lunch. Get it? *Ate a* . . . It rhymes with *data*."

"I'm sorry you're not feeling well, Dan," Mr. Vann says. "Hall pass is by the door, but . . ."

Mr. Vann waits a beat. Then the whole class buzzes.

"You cannot think of a word that rhymes with *data* because data is all around us," Mr. Vann says. He spreads his arms out wide and turns in a slow circle.

Dan throws his hands up. "Okay. How does that make any sense?"

"Chelsea," Mr. Vann says next. "Weather report, please."

Chelsea takes out her phone and taps the screen a few times. "Mostly sunny. High: sixty-eight. Low: fifty-two," she says.

Mr. Vann turns back to his huge chart. He writes **mostly sunny** in the box to the right of **1:12 p.m.** He writes **68 degrees Fahrenheit** in the next box, and **52 degrees Fahrenheit** in the last.

"We shall see," Mr. Vann says mysteriously. "We shall see." Then he sends us to our groups to generate some data of our own.

The Calculators meet up in our regular corner.

"So what should we do?" Dee Dee asks.

"Maybe something about April vacation?" Chelsea suggests. "We could make a survey about what people are planning to do and then graph it."

Dee Dee shrugs.

"You're right," Chelsea says. "Boring. Except for Mika. She gets to go to Florida again."

"Lucky duck," Dee Dee says.

"How about some data on what it would take to bring you guys with me?" I say. I know the idea is not very rational, practically imaginary, but it would be super fun.

"I think your basic credit card would do it," Dee Dee says. "Or a loan."

"The only things you should take out a loan for are houses, cars, and college," I say without thinking. It's one of my mom's rules. Anything else, she says, is really a "want" and not a "need."

"But what if you have an emergency?" Chelsea asks.

"You should have a rainy-day fund," I answer. "At least, that's what my mom would say."

"But you can't plan for everything," Dee Dee says with a shrug. "I mean, chaos theory and all that."

And even though Mr. Vann says that data is all around us, the Calculators can't seem to think of any at the moment.

When I get home from school, Grandma Beau is at the sink, washing dishes. I drop my backpack on the table.

"Where's Mom?" I ask.

Grandma Beau turns off the tap, wrings her hands on a dish towel, and turns around.

"She's resting," she says. "Bit of a difficult spell." Grandma Beau balls up the dish towel in her hands. Then she comes over to the table and pulls out a chair for me. She sits down. I do, too.

"Mika," she says matter-of-factly. But she doesn't say anything else.

I'm waiting for her to tell me that my mom is trying her best and that I need to be patient; that Mom's job now is to take care of herself and to get better, and our job is to help her do that; and that these things take time. But then Grandma Beau's shoulders crumple and she starts crying quietly. I don't think I've ever seen my Grandma Beau cry before.

She looks up and takes a deep breath. "Mika, listen," she says. "Your mother found a bump."

I have no idea what she's talking about. "What?" I say.

"A bump," Grandma Beau repeats, like saying it again will explain what she means.

"What?" I say again. And suddenly I feel like I'm shouting. "I don't know what you're talking about."

"Near the scar. It's like a lump. It's most likely nothing."

We haven't gotten to probability in math yet, so I don't know the exact meaning of *most likely,* but the look on Grandma Beau's face tells me that it is more likely a something than a nothing.

So even though they scooped out the bad spot on the peach, and then they scooped it again, there's a chance that a little bit of the badness stayed behind. And now it's a bump, or a lump. I don't know what the difference is. Maybe one is a surface and one is a solid.

I wonder exactly when my mom noticed it. I've seen her run her fingers over the scar millions of times. When did everything change?

I suddenly think of this silly movie that Mom and I watched once. A guy makes a deal with the devil to have all of his wishes come true. But his wishes keep getting messed up. He asks to be president of the United States so people will respect him. And he does get to be president, but it turns out he's Lincoln the night he goes to Ford's Theatre.

I know I said I wanted things to change. I wanted all this quiet and waiting and emptiness to end. I wanted it all to be over, but this is *not* what I meant. And if everything can change so suddenly and so randomly, maybe we should just stop pretending that there are any rules at all.

"I don't know what to do," Grandma Beau says. "We couldn't call over the weekend because it was, you know, the weekend. Well, we probably could have called, but your mom wasn't ready to call, but now it's Monday. . . ." Her voice trails off. "I can't force her to call, Mika. It's like she doesn't want to know."

"It's always better to know," I say, more to myself than Grandma Beau.

"It's not the end of the world," Grandma Beau says in a way that begs me to tell her she's right. She wipes her nose on her sleeve. "If it is something, you know, they'll just have to do another excision." She folds the dish towel in front of her. Then she shakes it out and folds it again.

"Another scoop out of the old peach," I say. And I wonder how many scoops you can take before there's no more peach left to scoop.

"But if it is something, Mika, it's . . ." Grandma Beau pauses for a minute. "It might be not so good."

I don't know exactly what she means by *not so good,* but I know close enough.

I stand up and walk to the fridge, but I don't open the door. Instead, I tear a piece of to-do-list paper off the magnet pad. Then I go into my mom's office and dial the phone. Katie answers.

"Hi, Mika," she says. "We can't wait to see you. Did you get your ticket?"

I don't tell her yet that I'm not coming.

"Is Dad there?" I ask.

My dad's at work, but Katie gives me the number and says she'll also text him. I call Jeannie and leave her a message, too. Then I call Chelsea. She picks up. Then I try Dee Dee. Her number goes straight to voicemail. Her sister's probably on the phone, but I know Dee Dee will call me back as soon as she can.

After a few minutes, the phone rings. I talk to Jeannie. As soon as I hang up, it rings again. It's my dad. And when I finally come out of the office, about twenty-one million phone calls later, I have my list.

I go to my mom's room and sit down on the side of her bed, gently.

Mom opens her eyes. "Mika," she whispers. She's lying on her side, curled up like a little kid trying not to have a nightmare.

"So," I start, "it looks like it's going to take a little longer to deal with all this than we first thought." I glance at my list. "Number one: I'm not going to Florida."

I get ready for the big explanation, to make my case and list my reasons, but Mom just nods.

"Number two: Dad has a colleague at the medical center here, and she can get you in for something called a PET scan. Dee Dee says it's sort of like a super-duper X-ray that shows"—I look down at my paper—"metabolic activity."

"Okay," Mom says blankly.

"You don't have to stay overnight," I say. "So Grandma Beau will bring you, and Jeannie will pick you up. But you won't be back before I get home from school. So number three: Dee Dee and Chelsea will come home with me on the bus that day. We'll make dinner for everybody. Just the girls."

Mom doesn't say anything, and for a second I wonder if she's even heard what I said. Then I hear her voice catch.

"Thank you, Mika," she says. And then, after a long moment, she asks, "Do we know right then?"

"It takes a day or two to interpret the data," I tell her.

And suddenly I wonder how much different next week will be from this week. Which direction are we traveling on this number line—positive or negative?

And then the question I really need to know the answer to becomes clear. "Mom," I say, "are you scared?"

She takes a deep breath. "Oh, my Mika-Mouse," she says.

I lean my forehead on her shoulder and let her hug me. I don't bother measuring how long it lasts. Then I just cry.

Math Journal Entry #23

Think of a question, any question.

Collect some relevant data to help you find the answer.

Explain your thinking using words, numbers, and/or pictures.

Question:

When will we know what's going on?

DATA

Day:	Tuesday
Time:	2:15 pm
Hours to get results:	24 - 48
Answer:	We should know by Thursday *

* (But I don't know WHAT we'll know.)

The next few days go by in a blur of pretending every-thing is normal. I wake up. I make my bed. I go to school. I come home. I do my homework.

Mr. Vann's data chart now takes up most of the board. He adds another entry at the bottom, and then tells us to interpret, interpret, interpret.

Looking at the chart, it's pretty easy to see that on chilly or rainy days, math starts right on time, if not a few minutes early. On nice days, math starts later and later.

"So what does the data tell us?" Mr. Vann asks. "What does it all mean?"

Dee Dee summarizes: "When it's nice outside, we're late, and when it's not, we're not."

"On this particular day"—Mr. Vann points to a Thursday where class started twenty-two minutes earlier than usual—"I presume we had a hurricane or possibly a tornado. I hope everyone made it through that extreme weather event unharmed." He pauses. "Although here it merely says: Overcast. High fifty-nine. Low forty-five. But as Dee Dee explained, when the weather is good, we arrive late. When the weather is bad, we arrive early. And on this day we arrived *very* early, so the weather must have been *very* bad." Mr. Vann raises an eyebrow and waits.

Chelsea flips through her day planner. "That was an early-dismissal day," she says. "It had nothing to do with the weather."

"Correct," Mr. Vann says. "Big data is big, and big data is data, but let us not be lured by its temptations. Let us not be confused by promises of exactitudes that do not exist. Let us not be coerced by correlations that may or may not be real. I remind you that no matter how clean your data, life is quite messy."

Mr. Vann closes his eyes and stays quiet, I guess to let the thought sink in. And I agree. Data is important, crucial even, but it doesn't give you the whole story.

I close my eyes, too. I get this picture in my mind of the person, whoever he or she is, whose job it will be to interpret my mom's scan results. That person will see tons of data about metabolic activity. That person will learn a whole lot about the cells in my mom's lower left extremity. But that person won't really know my mom.

I open my eyes when I hear the click, click, click of Principal Mir coming down the hallway. She walks into the room and stands by the door. Mr. Vann still has his eyes closed.

It's not like the class is misbehaving or anything. Even Dan is quiet. But it's not like we're *actually* doing anything, either. And I remember what Chelsea said way back when about how Mr. Vann might belong in an alternative school and not Highbridge Middle. Principal Mir's expression looks like she might be thinking the same thing.

After a few long minutes, I hear the click, click, click leave and fade away down the hall.

Mr. Vann pops his eyes open. "Who would like to share some data? For example, a survey that shows that nine out of ten people agree that caring is sharing."

"Sharing is caring," Dan corrects him.

"Yes, it is." Mr. Vann smiles.

A bunch of kids share their math journal entries as Mr. Vann walks around the room, this time with his eyes open.

Dee Dee shares the length of her sister's telephone conversations over the past week. "Due to some ongoing romantic drama at the high school," she explains, "there has been a definite uptick in phone minutes."

"Fascinating," Mr. Vann says from behind my desk. He takes a minute to peek over my shoulder at my math journal. Then he puts a sticky note on the page.

I don't know what I did to deserve any bonus points. I didn't collect very much data, and my data doesn't even help me answer the question I really need to answer. But when I look down, the sticky note says Googolplex. I don't know what googolplex is exactly, just that it's a really, really big number.

"Who's next to share?" Mr. Vann asks.

Chelsea raises her hand so high it looks like she's trying to touch the ceiling. "I *finally* made a birthday chart to keep track of the cupcakes. Better late than never. Then I turned the data into a pie chart, and then I turned the pie chart into an actual pie."

Chelsea points to a box on the counter.

"Three thousand billion bonus points!" Mr. Vann shouts. He reaches into his desk drawer and pulls out a pie cutter, some small paper plates, and a box of plastic forks. Again, how he fits all that stuff in there . . .

"I don't think three thousand billion is a real number," Dan says.

"Real numbers were covered in chapter two, Mr. Pimental," Mr. Vann says, running to the back of the room. He opens the box and starts slicing up the pie.

Dee Dee and Chelsea come home on the bus with me. When we get to my stop, I see Chelsea's mom waiting in her car on the corner. It reminds me of elementary school, when Mom used to drive out to the bus stop if it was raining or super cold.

"Hi, Mom!" Chelsea calls. She doesn't seem surprised to see her.

"Your mom's here?" I say. "You can't stay?"

Chelsea's mom gets out of the car and walks around to the trunk. "Hi, girls!" she calls to us. "I'll pick you up around seven, Chels."

Chelsea's mom opens the trunk and takes out a cooler, the kind you use for camping or a really big picnic. It has wheels and a handle to pull it. She sets the cooler on the sidewalk. Then she waves, gets back into her car, and drives away.

"Thanks, Mom!" Chelsea calls after her. "Ingredients," she says to me. "I couldn't lug everything to school with me, not with the pie."

"I'll get it," Dee Dee says. She drops her backpack, jogs over, and picks up the handle of the cooler. The back of her T-shirt today says: *Stand back. I'm going to try science.* Underneath the words, there's a picture of a huge explosion. I hope that's not a prediction for our dinner.

"You didn't have to do all that," I say to Chelsea.

"Yes, I did," she says. She picks up Dee Dee's backpack from the sidewalk and runs to catch up with her.

I look at the two of them ahead of me. I know sometimes I wish I could go back in time, to third grade or even just to the beginning of this year. But back then I thought Dee Dee was a kind-of-odd science geek and Chelsea was a slightly annoying Goody Two-shoes. I couldn't see all their sides and angles.

So I guess I was right about calculators after all. They are a handy support when you're working through a very long and complicated problem.

Math Journal Entry #24

Collect some data, any data.

Let your data paint a picture.

Then interpret what you see.

Today, Mr. Vann gives us an actual test from the actual textbook.

"Principal Mir insists," he says as he passes out the stapled packets. "Something about needing to know where we stand, although I believe I'm standing right here." He looks down at his feet.

Chelsea follows Mr. Vann around the classroom, passing out little baggies of cookies. "One to a customer," she says quietly.

"Dear thinkers," Mr. Vann announces, "please begin."

"The cookies or the test?" Dan says with a grin.

Mr. Vann nods seriously. "Both."

The test isn't just about data. It's about everything we've learned so far this year. I decide to start with the easy questions, and then move on to the more challenging ones. But *actually,* they all seem pretty easy.

The thing is the test just asks for the answers. You don't have to explain your thinking using words, numbers, and/or pictures. You don't have to embark on reflective discussions of math concepts. You only have to find the answer. It almost feels like cheating.

I'm done pretty quickly, and Mr. Vann has given us the entire math block, so I check my answers. I'm almost through my second round of attending to precision when I hear the ding-ding-ding of the PA system.

"Sorry for the interruption," Ms. Alice says, "but could you send Mika Barnes down to the office, please?"

At least she said my name correctly. But then I feel it, the clench at the back of my neck, like someone has grabbed me from behind. Dee Dee and Chelsea look up from their tests and over to me.

I was so lost in math that I'd *actually* forgotten. Today is the day my mom would probably get her test results. I guess the data has been interpreted. Now we know, and I suddenly don't know if knowing is always better.

"Oh, and have her stop by her locker and get her things," Ms. Alice adds. "She's going home early."

I stand and pick up my test. I walk over and hand it to Mr. Vann. He looks through the pages, scanning the answers. Then he flips back to the first page and skims through the entire test again. He pulls a red pencil from his desk drawer and writes *RM* in big bubble letters on the front.

"Mr. Vann?" Ms. Alice interrupts the silence.

My feet feel stuck to the floor. I don't want to go.

"She's on her way," Mr. Vann says.

I walk down the empty hallway. It feels like it takes forever to get to my locker. Another weird thing about time—the way it sometimes gets all pulled out like a piece of gum or a rubber band that stretches way more than you expect it to.

I fill my backpack. I don't know if we have a new math journal quandary, but I take my math journal just in case. I swing my backpack over my shoulder and close my locker.

When I get to the main office, Mr. B is standing outside the door. Today's tie has cats wearing tie-dyed vests and playing electric guitars. How does that tie exist in the same world where my mom is so sick?

"Oh, hi, Mika," Mr. B says, as if I've surprised him, as if it was my idea to come down to the office. "Got everything?"

I nod. I feel my throat tighten and my eyes get hot. I'm staring right at Mr. B's silly, silly tie. I want to strangle all of those stupid, ridiculous cats.

This is not where I want to be. I want to be back in Mr. Vann's class on a regular messed-up day, rolling my eyes at Dan P. or running to Quadrant Two or building three-dimensional figures out of marshmallows or eating Chelsea's fancy cupcakes.

If I can't stand what's going to happen in the future, then I'd rather just go back to the past. Back to when my biggest problem was wanting my own phone or worrying about what the Onesies were wearing.

I want to go back to doing the chapters in the right order. I want to go back to the world where two comes after one, and three comes after two, and four comes after three. Where if you follow the directions, the picture always turns out the right way.

I step into the main office. Ms. Alice has the phone in the crook of her neck as she waters plants on the windowsill. She gestures over to the waiting sofa with her chin.

There's Mom and Grandma Beau. I can tell from their faces that they've been crying.

"Mika." Mom looks up. I feel my own face crumble. I run over and collapse in her lap.

"Honey, it's good news," she says into my hair. "I'm sorry if we frightened you. I can't help the crying, but they're happy tears, Mika. Happy tears."

"It's nothing," Grandma Beau says, wiping her nose with the back of her sleeve. "Turns out it's nothing. So we're going out for lunch, and you're coming with us."

Mom picks up my backpack. "I will let you play hooky just this once," she says in her Mom-trying-to-be-cool way.

"Everybody else's parents let them," I say through my sniffles.

Jeannie meets us at the eggplant place.

"We should go to Paris to celebrate," she says.

The waitress brings us a stack of extra napkins since the ones on the table have already been used wiping eyes and noses. "You know, carpe diem and c'est la vie and all that," Jeannie says, blowing her nose with a loud honk.

I laugh. Like what are the chances of us actually going to Paris?

"I am totally serious," Jeannie says totally seriously. "I have more frequent flier miles than I'm ever going to frequently fly. Let's just go. Let's go now. Well, after the eggplant."

"I have school tomorrow," I say.

"And I don't think I'm quite up to that just yet," Mom says.

It's not like my mom is suddenly all better. What her clean scan means is that nothing has really changed. She'll still do her treatments. We will keep "watching and waiting," as her doctors say. It's the same-old-same-old, which is suddenly pretty great.

"Besides," Mom says, "Mika and I are saving Paris for when she graduates from high school. Right, Mika?"

"Right," I say with a nod.

Jeannie doesn't seem to be listening. She takes out her phone and starts tapping and swiping. "Let's just see, shall we? *Oh là là!*" She swoons. "This looks interesting. Not Paris, but it still might be, like, awesome." She does the last part in her best surfer-girl voice.

Jeannie hands her phone to Grandma Beau, who scrolls down and nods. "But it's Wednesday to Wednesday. Mika goes back to school on that Monday."

So much for that, I think. But then Mom surprises me. "I think missing a few days of school would be just fine," she says.

"I can finally shave!" I say a little too loudly.

"What?" Mom asks. She's totally confused.

"Kids these days," Jeannie says with fake disapproval.

"Okay," Grandma Beau says. She's tapping and clicking away at Jeannie's phone. "I have some points we can use, too. One benefit of being part of the digital economy." Grandma Beau gives Mom a look. Mom and I both roll our eyes.

Grandma Beau hands the phone back to Jeannie. "I need your password," she says.

Jeannie types in her password.

"Jeannie, dear," says Grandma Beau, "please don't tell me that your password is *password*."

Jeannie shrugs. "Wow, I have like twenty gazillion points."

"Twenty gazillion isn't a real number," I say.

"Well, I have elite status. Or platinum-supreme or something. Not sure. Too bad we don't have more people to bring along."

And that gives me an idea.

"Okay." Jeannie sighs. "It says this package is twenty thousand points per person. But . . . if we pay at least ten days in advance, there's a 10 percent discount, and kids under thirteen are free, but that's for the hotel portion only, not the flight. I am so confused."

I take my math journal out of my backpack to help Jeannie tackle this innovative problem and embark on a reflective discussion of this very relevant math challenge.

Unit 13

Probability

"We are most likely done with data," Mr. Vann announces. "At least, we probably are. And to increase the probability that we have enough time to start a new chapter on this final day before April vacation, we will possibly be moving to chapter five. I'd give it a seventy percent chance. If I were a betting man, I would almost definitely put my money on chapter five."

Mr. Vann starts writing a list of words on the board.

"Welcome, Principal Mir," he says suddenly, even though his back is to the door. Then he turns around with his usual flourish.

Principal Mir is not alone.

"Mr. Vann," she says formally. "May I introduce Ms. DeAngelis? She has been selected to take the reins for Grade Five Pod Two math next year."

I look at Dee Dee. Dee Dee looks at me. We both look at Chelsea. Chelsea's staring at the floor.

I can't believe they *actually* did it. I can't believe they fired Mr. Vann.

Was it because of the test? Was it because we didn't do well?

I thought I did fine, although I guess Mr. Vann never gave me an actual score. He just gave me an RM. But I'm sure Dee Dee knocked it out of the park, and I know Chelsea attended to precision, and Dan said the test was as easy as the pie that Chelsea brought in for her data representation, but not nearly as delicious.

I feel the words starting to bunch up in my throat. I need to tell Principal Mir that Mr. Vann is not the problem. Mr. Vann helps you with your problems, and not just your math problems. I raise my hand as high as I can.

"Hold that fine thought, dear Mika," Mr. Vann says to me. "Most delighted to meet you, Ms. DeAngelis," he says with a dramatic bow.

Mr. Vann seems surprisingly polite for someone getting fired and meeting his replacement.

And even though it's completely unlike her, Chelsea shouts out without even raising her hand. "But what about you?"

"Looping," Mr. Vann says mysteriously. He traces circles in the air with both index fingers.

"Loopy?" Dan asks. I can't believe he's *actually* here the day before a vacation.

"Loop-*ing*," Mr. Vann repeats. "Which is to say that we, dear thinkers, will be together for yet another go-round on this crazy carousel. We will meet again in September to begin the sixth-grade textbook. Or perhaps we will be ready to start the sixth-grade textbook right before summer. I always find the best time to start something new is right before a vacation. Don't you agree, Chelsea?"

Chelsea looks just as confused as the rest of us. Then she gets it. She smiles a huge smile. I get it, too.

Highbridge Middle needed to hire a new math teacher for Grade Five Pod Two because next year Mr. Vann will be teaching Grade Six Pod Two. Next year, he'll be teaching *us*.

Principal Mir shows Ms. DeAngelis to an empty seat in the back of the room.

"I'll leave Ms. DeAngelis to observe," Principal Mir says, adjusting the pencil behind her ear. "I'd like her to get a sense of how we do things here at Highbridge Middle."

Mr. Vann salutes, and then reaches into his desk drawer. He takes out a pile of spinners from the game Twister.

"One to a customer!" everyone shouts.

Math Journal Entry #25

Think of something, anything that can be considered as an experiment in probability. How would you express the likelihood of all the different possible outcomes?

Explain your thinking using words, numbers, and/or pictures.

Just the girls

Jeannie Katie Mom Chelseas Mom

Grandma Beau   Dee Dee   me   Chelsea

Our flight to **Orlando** on Wednesday has a 73% chance of an on-time arrival.

A canceled flight is a virtual impossibility.

However, there is a **1-in-10** chance that the flight will have a late departure.

There is a **1-in-6** chance that my place on the plane will be next to my (mom) and a **33%** chance that I will sit next to a member of

THE CALCULATORS

It is **100%** sure that we will have an ☆ AWESOME TIME. ☆ P=1.

It is also confirmed that Mr. Vann will be our math teacher again next year.

I think chances are low that math will be boring, and chances are ⬆high⬆ that we will continue our math journals.

(Good thing I have many pages left in mine.)

I would say there is a 50-50 chance that we will ever finish a textbook

There is still a possibility that my mom's cancer could come back.
But every day that passes, that probability goes down.

And I think chances are high
that whatever happens, we will be ☺K.

Mum and me

I can't give you exact numbers because, as you know by now, life is not exact.
Only math is.

Life is mostly estimation.

Acknowledgments

Innumerable thanks to:

Jennifer Weltz, whose dedication and energy require very large numbers to describe; Phoebe Yeh and the team at Crown for helping this story to grow exponentially; Dr. Mark Albertini at the University of Wisconsin for sharing his expertise and very valuable time; Jennifer Naalchigar for so thoughtfully rendering Mika's journal using words, numbers, *and* pictures; P.J. + N^2, always my #1 readers; all the outside-the-box educators I've had the privilege to learn from as a student, colleague, and parent; and my mom.

Author's Note

Solving for M is the story of one family's experience with the issues and emotions surrounding a melanoma diagnosis. The good news is that developments in melanoma treatment and specific considerations for melanoma patients are advancing at a rapid pace. Options and outcomes are better today than they were just a few years ago, and hopefully, someday very soon, this particular *M* will be completely solved.

About the Author

Jennifer Swender taught elementary school students for over a decade before turning to writing full time. She is the author of several picture books and early chapter books and develops curriculum materials for students and teachers. She once had a gig writing questions for math tests, which came in handy for Mr. Vann's math journal "explorations." Jennifer lives in Massachusetts with her family.

jacobsandswender.com

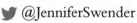 @JenniferSwender

About the Illustrator

Jennifer Naalchigar has been dreaming and doodling in her diaries from a young age—just like Mika. Unlike Mika, Jennifer showed limited promise in math, but she has thoroughly enjoyed exploring Mika's personality and reflecting her thoughts, fears, and dreams through her diary entries.

After working in publishing for several years, Jennifer turned her attention to illustrating full time and is now represented by the Bright Agency. She lives in Hertfordshire, England, with her husband and daughter.

@naalchidraws